Life Is Beautiful

HYPERION
MIRAMAX
B O O K S
NEW YORK

LIFE IS BEAUTIFUL

(LA VITA È BELLA)

ORIGINAL ITALIAN SCREENPLAY BY

ROBERTO BENIGNI AND VINCENZO CERAMI

english translation by Lisa Taruschio

ISBN: 0-7868-8469-X

Book design by Kathy Kikkert

First Edition
10 9 8 7 6 5 4 3 2 1

Life Is Beautiful

This is a simple story but not an easy one to tell. Like a fable, there is sorrow, and like a fable, it is full of wonder and happiness.

TITLE CARD
Arezzo, Italy
1919

Scene 1

Under a beautiful, crystalline sky, a Balilla convertible piled high with luggage makes its smooth, happy way through the placid Tuscan hills. FERRUCCIO, a plump young man with a jovial—almost boyish—look about him is driving. His friend, GUIDO, is in the passenger seat. He hugs the wheel as he recites lines of verse in a clear, bucolic tone.

FERRUCCIO

I sing what I see
Nothing gets by me.

He raises his voice as the car picks up speed, flying downhill.

FERRUCCIO

"Here I am," said I to chaos, "I am your slave!" "Good!" "For what," said I, "free in the end am I! What good is a caress when bliss...this man came to possess?"

"...Here I am, ready, the trains are gone, the brakes are gone and I can resist no more....Go sweet Bacchus, take me...the brakes are gone, oh..."

(*in a higher, worried voice*)
The brakes are gone!

His friend says, from under his hat,

GUIDO

I heard you!

FERRUCCIO

No, the brakes! They're really gone! Hit the brakes!

And he furiously kicks the dead brake pedal. At the first curve the car nearly goes off the road. Guido bounces like a spring and grabs the rolls of upholstery fabric, the car seats, the suitcases.

GUIDO

Weren't you reciting a poem?

FERRUCCIO

It doesn't work.

GUIDO

Brake! We're going to die! The woods! Brake!

Guido pulls the hand brake, but it's broken and nothing happens. Meanwhile, the car is gathering speed. It takes a sharp curve, goes off the road, and bounces down into a field, cutting the bushes in its path. Guido falls backward onto the upholstery rolls. A bump on the ground snaps the trunk open and two rolls of expensive fabric—one white, one gold—unravel and sweep the grass just as the car plunges into a tangled grove of thick flowering bramble bushes, ivy, and laurel, and comes out the other side completely covered in branches, leaves, and flowers.

The windshield is covered in twigs and leaves. Poor Ferruccio is now driving blind.

Guido stands up, holding on wherever he can, grabbing the windshield and looking ahead, trying to guide his friend.

Scene 2

———

A PAVED ROAD RUNNING THROUGH A VILLAGE—EXT., DAY

MAN #1

The king is coming.

WOMAN #1

There he is!

GUIDO

It's full of people down there.

In fact, beyond the long curve the road straightens and runs through a village where a local festival is in progress, complete with a band and Royalist and Fascist Youth banners and placards. When the crowd of locals, waiting in the shadow of a dais and holding placards that say LONG LIVE THE KING, see Guido and Ferruccio's extravagantly "decorated car" and the motorcycle escort approach, they begin to applaud. The band strikes up the Royal March, and adults and children salute the "king" as he passes.

Guido, his arm held high and stiff, shouts into the festive pandemonium.

GUIDO

We have no brakes! Move!

His gesture is mistaken for the Fascist salute. The villagers raise their arms and shout loud and strong, "Long live the king!"

The car, festooned with flowers and with its train of white and gold fabric, zooms through town and disappears into a curve at the bottom of the road. The crowd of villagers breaks onto the asphalt, saluting the car as it disappears and forcing the royal car, a convertible which has appeared (and in which are seated, in plain sight, His Majesty and the queen), to stop short. The king's chauffeur, honking the limousine's horn, drives the car slowly through the incredulous crowd.

Scene 3

A COUNTRY ROAD; A FARM—EXT., DAY

The Balilla, free of branches and colorful "drapings," stands dead under the sun in the middle of a dusty dirt road. Guido and Ferruccio are on their backs under the car, trying to repair the damage. Their voices are heard.

> FERRUCCIO *(from under the car)*
> Go for a walk. Otherwise we won't get there until tomorrow.

> GUIDO
> I found the screw. Now what do you need?

> FERRUCCIO
> Nothing, I need ten minutes alone.

> GUIDO
> All right, I'll leave you alone. Do you want the screw from before?

> FERRUCCIO
> No, I want to be alone.

> GUIDO
> Do I toss out the screw if I find it?

Guido, looking straight ahead as he walks away from the car, notices his black greasy hands.

> GUIDO
> I'm going to wash my hands.

There is an old farmhouse nearby, surrounded by an orchard and barn. Three cows, two white and one black, are tied to a fence. The black cow is next to a water pump. Guido walks up to the pump, hangs his coat and hat on a branch, and begins to pump water. Whistling, he fills a pail and washes his hands in the pail water, which immediately turns black. Nearby, a little girl is milking a white cow. Drying his hands in the air, Guido walks up to her. A horse is hitched to a wagon filled with baskets of vegetables and flowers. Guido, curious, takes a good look. He is happy, playful.

GUIDO

Hello, little girl. Where's your mother? Is she the one
who loaded this wagon?

ELEONORA

No, the landlady did.

GUIDO

Is it a market? Where's your mother? How old are you?
What's your name?

ELEONORA

Eleonora.

Guido bows graciously.

GUIDO

Nice to meet you, I'm Prince Guido!

ELEONORA

Prince?

GUIDO

Yes, I'm a prince. All this is mine, this principiant is the
prince's principiate. We'll name the place Addis Ababa.
Out with the cows, in with the camels!

ELEONORA

Camels?

GUIDO

Even a few hippopotamus! I have to go. I have an
appointment with the princess.

ELEONORA

When?

GUIDO

Now!

Someone cries out.

DORA'S VOICE

Ah!

Just above Guido's head, in the hayloft, a girl has been stung by a wasp. She loses her balance and falls out the window into Guido's arms as pigeons flap their way noisily out of the loft window. Guido and Dora fall down, rolling on straw. She is on top of him, a veil over her face.

GUIDO *(laughing)*

Good morning, Princess!

DORA

How frightening. I almost killed myself. Did I hurt you?

GUIDO

I've never been better. Do you always leave the house like this?

DORA

I was trying to burn out a wasps' nest...but I got stung.

She turns over onto her side. The veil falls from her face.

She rubs her thigh, just above her knee. Guido is lying next to her.

GUIDO

A wasp stung you? Here? Allow me! Hold still, Princess.

He takes her hand off her thigh, bends over, puts his mouth over the wasp sting. He sucks and spits.

GUIDO

You have to get the poison out right away, it's very dangerous!

Spits

Lie down, Princess.

Spits

It'll take a while.

Spits

Smiling, she backs away and stands up. He stands, too.

DORA

It's fine now, thank you.

GUIDO

Did you get stung anywhere else?

She picks her mosquito-net hat up off the ground.

DORA

No, thank you.

Looking up at the sky, Guido laughs.

GUIDO

What kind of place is this? It's beautiful: Pigeons fly, women fall from the sky! I'm moving here!

ELEONORA

It's all his! He wants to fill it with camels. He's a prince!

She approaches the pail. Dora is shy and embarrassed, but very curious about this frisky fellow.

GUIDO

Exactly. Prince Guido at your service, Princess!

With these words, he bows the deepest of bows. Dora smiles, while from the road the Balilla's horn sounds.

GUIDO
(*to Ferruccio*)

I'm coming!

GUIDO
(*to Dora*)

Good-bye then.

He puts his jacket on and hides a stick behind his back. He turns as he puts his hat on.

DORA

How can I thank you?

GUIDO

There's no need. If you really want to thank me I'll take some eggs to make a nice omelette for my squire.

DORA

Take whatever you want. It's all yours.

GUIDO

Thank you! I'll take two...six. All right! I'll make a nice omelette.

Then, as a farewell gesture, he raises his hat with the stick he has hidden behind his back.

GUIDO

Good-bye Eleonora. My regards, Princess. Farewell.

The horn sounds as the car starts moving. Guido walks quickly toward his friend, who is waiting behind the wheel.

GUIDO *(walking away)*
Here I am, Nuvolari....It's eggs for us tonight! All camels here!

The car is on its way again. Dora and Eleonora watch, smiling.

Scene 4

THE CITY; UNCLE'S HOUSE—EXT., NIGHT

Night has fallen. The Balilla crosses some city streets, a square, and enters a long boulevard. The car's headlights illuminate ancient monuments and some sinister images of the regime. Ferruccio's and Guido's voices are heard.

FERRUCCIO
Where is this house, anyway?

GUIDO
We're almost there. Turn left.

FERRUCCIO
Is your uncle sleeping here too with us?

GUIDO
No, he's been living in the hotel for thirty years. He's loaning us this house. He uses it for storage. There, we're here. That's my uncle's horse, Robin Hood. That's my uncle's buggy and that's my uncle's house. And he's inside.

Guido gets out of the car.

GUIDO
Hello dear uncle, here we are! Hurry, it's late. Here we are. The car broke down!

Before he finishes speaking, the front door suddenly bursts open. Guido is pushed backward and bumps into Ferruccio. Three young men hurriedly push their way out of Guido's uncle's house and run off, pushing Guido and Ferruccio out of their way and shouting.

GUIDO AND FERRUCCIO

Oh! What's happening? Who are they?

Guido hurries into the house, calling.

GUIDO

Uncle!

Ferruccio enters right behind him.

Scene 5

UNCLE'S HOUSE—INT., NIGHT

Guido's UNCLE is on the ground, disheveled and out of breath. He's trying to stand up. His nephew helps him.

GUIDO

Uncle!

His uncle wants no fuss. He stands up with a few groans of pain, but then smiles immediately.

UNCLE

Barbarians!

GUIDO

What happened. Who were those guys?

UNCLE

Never mind. Barbarians.

Meanwhile, Ferruccio is gathering up pieces of a broken vase. This isn't a house, it's a damp, cold warehouse. The old man is a collector of antiques, which are heaped carelessly in every room. Six or seven chandeliers hang from the ceiling, but only one is lit, and it lights up a bureau and assorted furniture covered with protective rags and blankets.

GUIDO
Are you hurt? Why didn't you cry for help?

UNCLE
Silence is the loudest cry! Come here, you two.

Guido's uncle is an elderly gentleman with a very refined manner and gestures. He is wearing a dark sport coat. He takes a long, hard look at Ferruccio.

UNCLE
This is your poet friend, right?

FERRUCCIO (intimidated)
Yes, I'm Ferruccio. I'm also an upholsterer.

UNCLE (moving)
Excellent! Come with me....all knickknacks here...an old passion that's a knickknack itself.

He pushes a switch and the light goes on in another room, which is also filled with old stuff. In one corner a double bed has been made.

FERRUCCIO
Madonna...what's all this stuff for?

Uncle pretends not to hear.

UNCLE
You can stay here as long as you like.

(to Guido)
I'll tell you right off, it's not easy to be a waiter! There's the bed. Legend says Garibaldi slept here.

He suddenly turns to Ferruccio.

                    UNCLE
Nothing is more necessary than the superfluous!

Then he turns toward his nephew as he opens the bathroom door.

                    UNCLE
The Town Hall is on Sestani Street, turn right after the
colonnade. You can go tomorrow morning. This is the
bathroom; with the appropriate invention of M. Bidet.

He closes the bathroom door and walks past a bookshelf.

                    UNCLE
There are a few books here, including a *Life of Petrarch* by
Lorenzo Paolino. The kitchen's there…and here's a
velocipede, commonly called a bike.

He goes toward the front door.

                    UNCLE
It's late, I have to get back to the hotel. There's only one
key, so don't lose it…it's hanging on the door. It's good
to see you. I'm coming, Robin Hood.

He goes outside.

                    FERRUCCIO *(admiringly)*
What an uncle!

Scene 6
_____

THE CITY; LOCAL STREETS—EXT., DAY

*A sunny morning. Guido and Ferruccio are walking through the city. They are happy
and full of hope. Their heads turn left to right as they observe everything. Every now
and then, Guido does a funny step.*

GUIDO

No one pays attention here. Isn't it great? If you feel like
doing something, you do it. You want to let yourself go,
you want to yell? Yell!

Ferruccio doesn't wait to be asked twice: He suddenly shouts, at full throat,

FERRUCCIO *(shouts)*

Eeeeeh!

Several heads turn, startled.

GUIDO

What're you, crazy? You think you're in the country
where you can do as you please? This is the city!

You've been yelling like a madman for three hours! You
can't yell.

*Just then, a man in work clothes with a basket of fruit in hand shouts up at an open
window on the third floor of the building.*

WORKMAN *(shouting)*

Maria! The key!

*A second later the enormous key to the front door falls from above, almost landing on
the two friends, who get out of the way just in time.*

GUIDO

You see? You can't yell.

Scene 7

UPHOLSTERY SHOP—INT., DAY.

*Twins six or seven years of age are bouncing on an old, broken-down sofa. It is a nice
upholstery shop, filled with fabric, cushions, drapery, rugs, and mattresses. The owner*

is tall and hardy, a good-natured man. Guido and Ferruccio are standing in front of him, paying attention to what he's saying.

UPHOLSTERER *(to Ferruccio)*
If you got all that poetry out of your head you'd make your
father very happy and you'd make more money than he!

GUIDO
Right, Oreste! That's what I keep telling him—you have
to settle down.

He spies a handsome hat on the counter, takes his own off, and puts the other on.

GUIDO
How does it look on me?

The upholsterer puts the hats back where they belong.

UPHOLSTERER
Nice, but it's mine!

FERRUCCIO
So when do I start work?

UPHOLSTERER
Right now. You're already late.

He points to an armchair.

UPHOLSTERER
Take that chair down to the workshop.

When he turns, Guido exchanges the hats again.

GUIDO
I'm going to the Town Hall. See you later.

He extends his hand to the upholsterer for a handshake, tipping his hat slightly.

The upholsterer laughs, stops him, and exchanges the hats again. Guido's own hat is back on his head.

UPHOLSTERER

Yeah, see you later. And behave yourselves. These are hard times, very hard.

GUIDO

Hard times, huh?

Ferruccio is moving the armchair.

GUIDO

What do you think of the political situation?

Just then the twins pull a curtain down.

UPHOLSTERER

Benito! Adolf! Behave!

He turns to Guido.

UPHOLSTERER

What did you say?

GUIDO

Uh, I was saying—okay, okay, so long!

Ferruccio is pulling an armchair along the floor. The upholsterer turns to him.

UPHOLSTERER

You'll break the legs that way.

Guido sneaks another hat change, and leaves the shop with the upholsterer's hat on his head.

GUIDO

See you later!

The upholsterer turns, suspicious, and sees Guido's old hat on the counter instead of his own new one. He grabs it and runs to the door, but he is too late. He returns inside the shop with an evil grin.

UPHOLSTERER
He got away with it! But I'll find him.

He turns
Benito, you're going to get a smack!

Scene 8

TOWN HALL—INT., DAY

It is a large office on the second floor of a small building, with two large open windows that overlook the street. Flowerpots are on the windowsill. Guido is seated in front of the secretary's desk. She is a polite, older woman. She dips her pen into the inkwell.

GUIDO
I would like to fill out all the necessary forms to open a bookstore. Will it take long?

SECRETARY
Years.

GUIDO
So we better start now.

SECRETARY *(checking her watch)*
Now? It's nearly one, we're closing soon. Come back this afternoon.

GUIDO
I can't, my uncle has to give me waitering lessons.

SECRETARY

Then come back tomorrow. In the meantime, you have
to fill out a formal application which our town clerk has
to sign....

*She gestures toward the door behind her, beyond which is a young man who is putting
on his jacket, getting ready to leave. Guido stands up, but as he moves he remembers
that the eggs from yesterday are still in his pockets. He takes them out slowly.*

GUIDO

Oh, Lord, the eggs. We nearly had a real omelette here.

Holding three eggs in his hand, he keeps talking to the secretary.

GUIDO

Fill it out, we'll get him to sign right away. Write: The
undersigned, Orefice, Guido, hereby applies...

SECRETARY *(interrupting)*

But he can't sign it immediately!

*The town clerk, hat on his head and briefcase in hand, comes out of his office. It is DR.
RODOLFO, an elegant young man with broad shoulders and a smiling, congenial
air about him.*

GUIDO

Here he is, here he is!

DR. RODOLFO

What's going on here?

He is about to speak to the secretary, but Guido butts in.

GUIDO

I need your signature to open my bookstore.

Rodolfo stares at the stranger with eggs in his hand and turns to the secretary.

DR. RODOLFO
Signorina, what is going on?

SECRETARY
Dr. Rodolfo, I told him, but he insists!

GUIDO
Dr. Rodolfo, one little signature!

DR. RODOLFO
I can't. My replacement will be here in an hour, ask him.

GUIDO
But it's just a signature, right?

DR. RODOLFO
We close at one. Got it?

He turns and strides out. Guido looks at the clock.

GUIDO
But it's only ten to one!

DR. RODOLFO
File a complaint!

With the town clerk gone, Guido, eggs still in hand, goes to the window and says to the secretary,

GUIDO
Okay, I'll file a complaint. The undersigned, Orefice,
Guido...
(*He changes tone*)
What a nasty guy, huh? So when is his replacement due?
Jes—

Leaning on the windowsill, he accidentally overturns one of the flowerpots, which falls out the window. He looks out....

Scene 9

The flowerpot, dropping from the second floor, falls smack on Rodolfo's head as he exits the town hall doors. He staggers, his head covered in soil.

> GUIDO
>
> Jesus, what a hit!

And he runs to help Rodolfo, who is stunned. His hat has fallen off his head, landing upside down on a nearby low wall, and his hair and jacket are covered in soil, leaves, and flowers. Guido runs up to him.

> GUIDO
>
> I'm really sorry. Are you hurt? I didn't do it purposely, I just leaned, and...I'm really sorry...

He wants to help. But he has the six eggs in his hands. Quickly, he puts them inside Rodolfo's hat on the low wall and starts brushing dirt off the town clerk's jacket and hair.

> DR. RODOLOFO *(furious)*
>
> I'll do that myself! And you can kiss your bookstore good-bye, my good man!

But Guido keeps brushing soil off Rodolfo's jacket while the latter, watching Guido with revenge in his eyes, reaches for his hat.

> GUIDO
>
> No! The eggs!

But it's too late: Sticky, yellowish raw egg spills from under the hat onto Rodolfo's ears and face. Instinctively, Guido steps back, while the town clerk watches him with a poisonous look.

> DR. RODOLFO
>
> You good-for-nothing! I'll kill you!

He makes a grab for Guido, who runs like hell.

Guido spots a man ahead on a bicycle, leading a riderless bike with one hand. Without missing a beat, Guido makes a straddle jump onto the empty bike seat and pedals off madly. The man realizes too late what has happened; he stops, shocked, and gets off his bike, watching as the thief disappears beyond a curve, pedaling at full speed.

> MAN WITH THE BICYCLE *(yelling)*
> Hey, that's mine, what're you doing?

Before he can yell, "Stop, thief!" another guy comes along and snatches his bike. It is Rodolfo, who jumps onto the seat and pedals after Guido. The man goes running after the two thieves, shouting at the top of his lungs.

Scene 10

CITY STREETS—EXT., DAY

Guido turns a corner and stops short so as not to hit a line of children being shepherded across the street by their teacher. The bike skids and turns over on its side. Guido misses the children but winds up colliding with the teacher, who is none other than the pretty young Dora he met at the little farm. She is thrown in the air, and this time it's Guido who lands on top.

> GUIDO *(smiling)*
> Good morning, Princess!

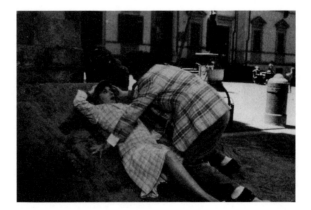

He stands up under her astonished gaze.

GUIDO

Maybe someday we'll meet standing up! Sorry—gotta run.

He runs off at full speed while Dora, somewhat amazed and somewhat amused, gets to her feet.

Scene 11

THE GRAND HOTEL—INT., DAY

It is morning. In the huge, luxurious lobby of the Grand Hotel, the staff is busy cleaning: dusting, polishing, arranging flowers, brushing the sofas, pushing breakfast carts toward the service elevators.

Guido walks quickly down the main staircase. As he walks, he is putting on his tight, sleek tuxedo jacket. His shirt is buttoned wrong, his tie is undone. He walks toward his uncle, who sees him and sits down at a table set with a tray holding a bottle of champagne and two glasses. Buttoning his shirt, Guido stops in front of his uncle.

UNCLE

Chicken!

GUIDO

Easy! Chicken is served whole, on its back on the plate. "Would you cut it for me?" "Of course!" First, I hold the chicken down with the knife blade stuck under its wing and rip off the drumstick. Then I slice the meat along the breastbone. Off go the wings and breast, off goes the skin....

His uncle, satisfied, interrupts.

UNCLE

Lobster!

Panic flashes in the apprentice waiter's eyes.

> GUIDO
>
> I stick the skin under the wing...off goes the leg, I rip off the lobster...stick the...lobster is a crustacean. Off with the crust....

(He hesitates.)

> ...Off with the antennae, off goes the lobster. There's nothing left. We're out of lobster but we have some delicious chicken.

His uncle watches, puzzled.

> GUIDO
>
> I don't remember lobster, Uncle.

> UNCLE
>
> Lobster is served just as it comes out of the kitchen. You don't touch it.

> GUIDO
>
> Too easy, that's why I didn't remember.

> UNCLE
>
> Go on!

Guido pretends he is a page at court: With his back arched, he minces around his uncle, mimicking the movements of a good waiter.

> GUIDO
>
> Behavior. Stand by. Still, like this. "Waiter!" "Yes?" In position, stand-by behavior. "Waiter!" Why are they all calling me? There must be other waiters, right?

> UNCLE
>
> Champagne!

He hops around like a waiter called to serve several tables. He stops a moment to think.

His uncle watches, stunned. Guido starts going through various kinds of bows.

> GUIDO
>
> The bow is simple! Hands on hips…lower the torso…and…and you swing down like a bottle of champagne. Forty-five degrees…er, fifty…no…

He bows, literally, in half.

> GUIDO
>
> No! More than ninety degrees! At right angles! Let's show how…Okay, Uncle, what's the degree for a proper bow?

His uncle shakes his head and stands up.

> UNCLE
>
> Look at sunflowers bowing to the sun. If you see one bowed too low, it means it's dead. You are serving, but you're no servant!

Uncle approaches his nephew, who is still bowed low.

> UNCLE
>
> Serving is the highest art. The Lord is the first servant….

Fondly, he starts tying his nephew's tie.

> UNCLE
>
> God serves men but he's not a servant to men!

Uncle sticks his finger under Guido's collar.

> GUIDO
>
> There's no button here.

> UNCLE
>
> It doesn't go there, silly!

Smiling, he gives his nephew a light smack on the head. Then he takes the bottle of champagne and shakes it.

Scene 12

UNCLE'S HOUSE—INT., NIGHT

The two friends are in bed, one next to the other, in pajamas. A lamp is lit, but on an old table against the far wall. Ferruccio seems worried, his head resting on the pillow.

> FERRUCCIO
> I have to bring the car back to my father, he's counting on it.

> GUIDO
> In a month.

> FERRUCCIO
> No, I promised I'd bring it back sooner. You know why?

He stops.

> GUIDO
> Why?

Ferruccio doesn't answer, and Guido, worried, pokes him.

> GUIDO
> Ferruccio?

Ferruccio awakes from a deep sleep, and looks around, frightened.

> FERRUCCIO
> What is it? What time is it?

GUIDO

What are you talking about? We were talking a moment
ago....Were you sleeping?

FERRUCCIO

Of course I was sleeping!

GUIDO

You asked me a question, turned your head, and went to
sleep. How did you do that?

FERRUCCIO

Schopenhauer!

GUIDO

Who?

FERRUCCIO

Schopenhauer says that with will, you can do anything:
"I am what I want," and right now I want to be asleep. So
I say to myself, "Sleep, sleep, sleep!" And I'm asleep.

Excited, Guido pays attention.

GUIDO

Nice. Simple.

*He moves his fingers, conjuring something to come to him, and his voice gets deep and
mysterious.*

GUIDO

Sleep, sleep, sleep.

FERRUCCIO (*annoyed*)

Stop moving your hands, you're not a juggler. This is real
serious stuff, it takes time! Okay, good night, we'll talk
about it tomorrow.

Guido is puzzled. But Ferruccio falls asleep instantly. So Guido practices the theory: He moves his fingers above his sleeping friend's face.

> GUIDO
>
> Wake up, wake up…
>> *(He raises his voice.)*
>
> Wake up!

Ferruccio opens his eyes with a start, frightened.

> FERRUCCIO
>
> What is it? What are you doing?

> GUIDO *(excited)*
>
> Wow, it works.

> FERRUCCIO
>
> What works?

> GUIDO
>
> Schopenhauer! I said, "Wake up, wake up," and you woke up right away! The will is incredible. How does it all happen?

> FERRUCCIO
>
> It happens that you woke me up. You were yelling "Wake up" into my ear, so of course, I woke up!

> GUIDO
>
> You mean I should say it lower.

> FERRUCCIO
>
> No, don't say it at all! It's deep—you have to think it.

Ferruccio turns his back and closes his eyes again. Guido tries to think his friend awake again.

Scene 13

THE CITY; A PIAZZA AND A BAR—EXT., DAY

The city is sunny and festive. Ferruccio walks in long strides. Guido, behind him, can barely keep up.

> GUIDO
> Take it easy, where are you going?

> FERRUCCIO
> I'm late!

They pass the same workman, in his overalls, with a basket of fruit in one hand. He is looking up at the third floor.

> WORKMAN
> Maria! The key!

From the third floor window, someone throws the heavy key, which lands on Guido's shoulder, nearly knocking him over.

> GUIDO
> Ow!

> WORKMAN
> Sorry!

Guido runs toward Ferruccio, laughing.

> GUIDO
> Every day he has someone throw down the key. It nearly hit me in the head!

Scene 14

THE CITY STREETS—EXT., DAY

Two women are walking nearby: Dora and her friend ELENA, who is also a schoolteacher.

> GUIDO
>
> Look! That's the teacher. Boy is she pretty. I even dreamt about her. Come on, I'll introduce you.

As they approach the women, Guido stops and hides behind Ferruccio, who stops dead, still as a statue.

> GUIDO
>
> Holy smokes! Stay still.

> FERRUCCIO
>
> What?

Rodolfo, the town clerk, has stopped his car, and gotten out. He is past the two men and is approaching the women, who greet him enthusiastically.

> GUIDO
>
> Stop. That's the jerk the eggs fell on, the town clerk. Stop! If he sees me he'll kill me. Now what's he doing? Did he leave?

Guido's face is up against the back of Ferruccio's neck. Ferruccio is standing absolutely still, watching the two women and the clerk.

> FERRUCCIO
>
> No, he's there, he's talking.

> GUIDO
>
> What's he saying?

> FERRUCCIO
>
> How should I know?

What's he doing?

FERRUCCIO

He's saying good-bye. He's leaving. He's got a car just
like mine.

*Rodolfo kisses both women on the cheek. On his way back to his car, he passes
Ferruccio.*

FERRUCCIO

Here he is!

GUIDO

Don't move! He'll kill me if he sees me.

*The car, which is made by the same manufacturer and is the same color as Ferruccio's
(but shiny and clean), moves off. Dora and Elena start walking toward Ferruccio,
who, embarrassed, doesn't move. He still has not caught his breath. As the women come
to the "statue," they stop for a moment, just in time for Guido to pop out from behind
his friend.*

GUIDO

Good morning, Princess.

He takes his hat off.

Dora is surprised and amused. Elena is frightened.

Dora laughs and looks at Guido as if he were a magician.

DORA

It's you—again. How do you do it?

Guido introduces Dora to Ferruccio.

GUIDO

This is the princess who fell into my arms from the sky!

Elena figures out who Guido is.

> ELENA
> Oh—is he the one who sucked the stinger out of your thigh?

> DORA
> Yes, yes!

She says happily to Guido.
> Do you always appear out of nowhere? We always meet like this....

> GUIDO
> Next time we can plan it. How about tonight at eight?

> DORA (*smiling*)
> No, this way's nicer.

> ELENA
> Come on, Dora, you'll be late for school.

> DORA (*to Guido*)
> I hope we run into each other again—by chance. 'Bye!

> GUIDO
> Farewell, Princess!

Walking quickly, the two women go on their way.

> GUIDO (*to Ferrucio*)
> Did you see her? She's pretty. She likes it when I suddenly appear.

Scene 15

THE GRAND HOTEL—INT., NIGHT

It is the middle of the night. In the hotel lobby only a few lights are lit. There is hardly anyone around. Guido, wearing his tuxedo, comes out of the kitchen holding a tray and walks to the bar where there is only one customer: DR. LESSING, a middle-aged German with an easy-going, vaguely intellectual air. He is seated at a table sipping a glass of cognac.

Guido, tray in hand, stops before the German, looks at him, and smiles. Dr. Lessing understands immediately.

                    DR. LESSING
I don't believe it!

                    GUIDO
"Obscurity."

                    DR. LESSING
Guido, you're a genius.

                    GUIDO
"The more there is, the less you see it!" Answer:
"Obscurity!" It's great! Did you make the riddle up
yourself, doctor?

                    DR. LESSING
No, but you solved it in five minutes, it took me eight
days. Obscurity.

Guido puts the tray down on the table.

                    GUIDO
Here we are!

The familiarity and affability between waiter and guest are evident. Guido indicates the plates on the tray.

GUIDO

Salmon, salad, and a glass of white wine.

DR. LESSING *(concentrating hard)*

Listen to this one, Guido.

Guido stops him.

GUIDO

If I may, it's my turn! I learned this one as a kid: "Snow
White and the seven dwarfs sit down for a bite. How fast
can you guess what she serves her guests next?"

*He smiles smugly. Dr. Lessing picks up his pen and writes the riddle down, repeating it
as he writes.*

DR. LESSING *(translating into German as he writes)*

It sounds refined. I want to solve it right away.

GUIDO

Eat first or it'll get cold.

Dr. Lessing looks at the tray and wrinkles his nose.

DR. LESSING

Guido, I'm sorry, it looks very good, but I can't, it's too
late.

GUIDO

What? Salmon, salad, white wine...it's a light supper.

DR. LESSING *(thinking out loud)*

"Snow White and the seven dwarfs..."

The NIGHT PORTER, in uniform, walks up behind Guido and says in a low voice,

NIGHT PORTER

Guido!

Guido goes to him.

NIGHT PORTER

Is the kitchen closed?

GUIDO

Everyone's gone, why?

NIGHT PORTER

There's a gentleman just arrived from Rome, from the ministry. He wants to eat.

GUIDO

The kitchen's closed.

NIGHT PORTER (*whispering*)

Too bad. He's a good tipper.

GUIDO

The kitchen's open. Show him in, where is he?

He is standing a few steps from the night porter: it is an INSPECTOR from the Ministry of Public Education. He has a pile of files under his arm; his glasses rest on the tip of his nose. He has a strict air about him, and carries a raincoat and hat in his hand. Guido goes to meet him and shows him to a table in the bar.

GUIDO

Please, sit down!

He seats him at a table with his back toward Dr. Lessing. Then he goes quickly to the doctor's table.

GUIDO

You're sure you don't want to eat anything?

Dr. Lessing sips his cognac, his head is in the clouds.

DR. LESSING

No, no! "Snow White and the seven dwarfs…"

Guido returns to the inspector's side.

INSPECTOR

I know the kitchen's closed, but maybe you could find
something for a cold supper...

GUIDO

Leave it to me! Pick whatever you like, everything's
delicious!

INSPECTOR

Something light.

GUIDO

Well, we have...meat: a nice rich steak, or lamb, or
kidney, breaded, fried liver...tough...or fish.

INSPECTOR

Fish, fish!

GUIDO

Good. How about a nice, fatty turbot? Or eel stuffed
with fatty sausage and greased with Grand Marnier? Or
some lean salmon. Whatever you'd like.

INSPECTOR

The salmon. Thank you.

GUIDO *(interrupts him)*

Side dish?

INSPECTOR

There's a side dish too?

GUIDO

Feel free to choose. We have very, very, very fried
mushrooms, Nancy buttered potatoes with a creamy
sauce.

The inspector looks nauseated.

> INSPECTOR
>
> Don't you have a simple, light salad? If not, forget it.

> GUIDO
>
> A light salad? Too bad; the very fried mushrooms are out of this world. So: steamed salmon and salad, and a glass of white wine.

> INSPECTOR
>
> Perfect!

He looks at his watch.

> As soon as possible.

> GUIDO
>
> I'll do my best.

Guido goes to Dr. Lessing, takes the tray that is on the table and puts it down in front of the Inspector who, reading the papers, is amazed, so amazed that, thinking he has lost all sense of time, he looks at his watch. Meanwhile, Dr. Lessing has stood up and is going toward the stairs. He stops near Guido and looks him straight in the eye.

> DR. LESSING
>
> "How fast can you guess what she served her guests next..."

> GUIDO
>
> Right!

> DR. LESSING
>
> Good night.

He climbs the stairs, repeating the riddle to himself.

> INSPECTOR (*to Guido*)
>
> What did he say? Snow White? What, is he drunk?

GUIDO

No, it's a riddle: "Seven seconds." Seven seconds is the
solution time. Snow White and the seven dwarfs. If there
are seven dwarfs dining and she serves seconds, that
means seven seconds. Dr. Lessing is a physician, a very
serious person. But he's obsessed with riddles, he loses
sleep over them.

Guido notices a red, white, and green sash folded on top of the Inspector's files.

INSPECTOR

Excuse me, the Francesco Petrarca elementary school...

GUIDO

It's not far from here. A friend of mine teaches there.
Great school.

INSPECTOR

Good, so I can sleep an extra half hour.

As he eats, he looks through his files.

GUIDO

You have to be there tomorrow morning?

INSPECTOR

Yes, they're expecting me at eight-thirty.

He returns to the inspector.

GUIDO

So, tomorrow morning, you're going to the school....

The inspector turns and looks at Guido.

INSPECTOR

Yes. I'm visiting the classes.

GUIDO

Visiting all the classes. Well. Good, good. You'll have some good advice for the children. You'll check everything out.

The inspector finishes his meal and drinks the wine.

INSPECTOR

More or less. That's my job, I'm an inspector.

GUIDO

An inspector's an important person. So you have to be at the school at eight-thirty tomorrow.

INSPECTOR

Right. And now I'm going to bed. Thanks for the excellent meal.

He stands up and takes his things.

GUIDO

I'll show you the way.

He picks up the inspector's raincoat, hat, and tricolor sash. The inspector takes his briefcase. They move to the elevator. Guido gives the inspector his raincoat and hat.

GUIDO

Here you are.

INSPECTOR

Oh, I forgot—I'd like a wake-up call at seven, not a minute earlier, not a minute later. Good night.

GUIDO

Good night.

The elevator door closes. Guido turns and goes quickly to the night porter. In his hands, which are behind his back, he is carrying the inspector's tricolor sash. At the night desk, Guido says to the night porter,

Wake-up call for him at nine! Not a minute earlier, not a minute later.

He leaves.

Scene 16

FRANCESCA PETRARCA ELEMENTARY SCHOOL—CLASSROOM
INT.–EXT., DAY

A large classroom. The children, all dressed up in clean, pressed uniforms, are sitting somewhat intimidatedly, at desks arranged to form a large "M." The school's teachers and administrators are standing behind tables that make up the dais; there is an elderly lady PRINCIPAL, the SECRETARY, several TEACHERS (Dora among them).

PRINCIPAL
Please, children, silence! A moment of attention. The inspector from Rome will be here shortly. I want to make a good impression on him. Listen very quietly and carefully to what he says. He'll tell us some very important things about our beautiful country.

A MAN IN A SUIT runs past the students towards the principal.

MAN IN A SUIT
The inspector is here, ma'am.

PRINCIPAL
He's already here? He's early! Sit down, Roberto!

The inspector's loud, sure footsteps are heard. The children are quiet. Guido, wearing the red, white, and green sash draped over one shoulder and running between his legs, makes his entrance.

PRINCIPAL
All rise!

The children jump to their feet in unison. Guido walks past the students as they stand, and strides toward the teachers. Dora sees him and is astonished.

GUIDO *(to Dora)*

Good morning, Princess.

PRINCIPAL

Good morning, Mr. Inspector. I'm the principal. These are some of our teachers.

GUIDO

Good.

Guido begins shaking hands with each teacher. The first one is DORA'S FRIEND.

GUIDO

So…how many years have you taught in this school district?

DORA'S FRIEND

Sixteen.

GUIDO *(to a male teacher)*

GUIDO

And are you up to date with the ongoing school program approved by the ministry this year?

MALE TEACHER #1

Yes.

GUIDO *(to a female teacher)*

Did you read the bulletin regarding childhood hygiene?

FEMALE TEACHER #1

Of course!

GUIDO *(to Dora)*

What are you doing on Sunday?

DORA

What?

GUIDO

No, I mean, Sunday...is St. Mary's Day. What are you
doing?

DORA

I'm going to the theater.

GUIDO

To see what?

DORA

Offenbach.

GUIDO

Right. They're playing Offenbach. Fine. Well...

GUIDO *(to Principal)*

Thank you very much and good-bye. I just came to...

PRINCIPAL

We know.

PRINCIPAL *(to the group)*

As you know, the inspector came from Rome to talk to us
about the race manifesto signed by the most enlightened
Italian scientists.

She points to the poster on the wall, which Guido scans rapidly.

PRINCIPAL

He will, and we're very honored, demonstrate to us that
our race is a superior, race—the best of all!

Take your seats.

The children sit down.

Go ahead, Inspector.

GUIDO

Our race, as we know…

PRINCIPAL

…is superior!

GUIDO

Naturally! Our race is superior. I've just come from Rome, right this minute, to tell you in order that you'll know, children, that our race is a superior one. I was chosen, I was, by racist Italian scientists in order to demonstrate how superior our race is.

In a flash, he jumps up on the table to show the children how handsome he is.

GUIDO

Why did they pick me, children? Must I tell you? Where can you find someone more handsome than me? Justly so, there is silence. I'm an original "superior race"—pure Aryan. Children, let's start with something that one says, "What's so big about that?" The ear.

He shows his left ear to the children.

GUIDO

Look at the perfection of this ear. Left auricle with a
pendant little bell at the end. Check it out! Movable
cartilage! Bendable! Find two ears more beautiful than
these and I'll leave! But you have to show me them! They
dream about these in France. Races exist, children. You
bet they do! But let's continue. I want to show you
something else.

He begins to remove his jacket.

GUIDO

Pay attention.

Scene 17

FRANCESCA PETRARCA SCHOOL—HALLWAY INT., DAY

The inspector and the man in a suit walk quickly down the hall.

INSPECTOR

He said "inspector"? From Rome?

Scene 18

FRANCESCA PETRARCA SCHOOL—CLASSROOM INT., DAY

*Guido in shorts and his undershirt, the tricolor sash looped over his shoulder and run-
ning between his legs (accentuating everything), stands on the desks, which are
arranged in an "M" amongst the children. His undershirt is up around his belly, which
he is showing to the children.*

GUIDO

The belly button! Take a look at this belly button! What
a knot! But you can't untie it, not even with your teeth!
Those racist scientists tried. Not a chance! This is an
Italian belly button. It's part of our race!

*He parades up and down the "M," showing his belly button to the children, then stops
and shows off his arm muscles.*

GUIDO

Check out this style! Look at these muscles: ceps, biceps,
triceps! Look at this beauty! Admire this hip!

Guido dances on the desks.

GUIDO

Just look at the movement! Gentlemen!

*The inspector, standing in the doorway, can't believe his eyes. Guido spots him and
quickly gathers up his clothes from the windowsill.*

GUIDO

I must say good-bye now, because I have to go, I have an
appointment. I'll make my Aryan exit and bid you
farewell. Farewell!

Guido jumps onto a windowsill and lifts his shirt, revealing his belly button.

GUIDO

The belly button!

Clothes in hand, he's about to jump out the window. But first he turns to Dora.

GUIDO

I'll see you in Venice, Princess!

He jumps out the window.

Scene 19

It is the fourth act of The Tales of Hoffmann.

Scene is Venice at night. On the water, silver in the moonlight, a gondola carries Juliette and Nicklaus. They are singing the heartrending "Belle nuit d'amour."

Dora, her face lit by the reflection from the stage, is sitting in one of the orchestra boxes. She is rapt in the music. Her friends, seated behind her, are also spellbound by the performance. Elena is there with a male friend; so is Rodolfo and another young man.

The entire audience is enthralled by the performance before their eyes. Only one person is not looking at the stage; he is turned toward an orchestra box. It is Guido, entranced by the lovely Dora. At his left, consulting the libretto in the dim light, is Ferruccio. At his right is an UNKNOWN WOMAN. She is not beautiful but, seeing how uninterested Guido is in the performance, and that he is turned in her direction, she watches him with an intent, puzzled expression. Guido smiles quickly and points to his left ear.

> GUIDO *(in a whisper)*
> I hear only with this ear.

The lady relaxes and sits back to enjoy the opera. The two singers are at the end of the piece. Gently rocked by the low waves of the lagoon, they sing the finale of the Barcarole.

Dora listens closely, her eyes moist with emotion. Guido watches her and, waving the fingers on both hands slightly, murmurs something.

> GUIDO *(murmuring)*
> Look at me, Princess—I'm here. Turn around...
> *(He raises his voice slightly.)*
> Turn around, turn around....

Dora moves slightly, as if prodded by an invisible force.

Guido concentrates harder, moves his fingers more quickly.

GUIDO

Turn, turn...

Ever so slowly, she turns. Guido is in seventh heaven, his face frozen in a smile of ecstasy. The lady next to him has turned to him, and this time she smiles at him, perhaps with a pinch of malice. Guido comes to his senses, a little frightened, and finally turns his attention to the stage and the hypnotic beauty of the opera.

Scene 20

THEATER—EXT., TWILIGHT

The full-house matinee performance is over. The spectators, leaving the theater, find that the sky has darkened and it is pouring rain. The crowd is thickest at the theater doors; a few umbrellas open. Some people risk the downpour, running for the covered portico or to get their cars.

Scene 21

THEATER, CORRIDOR, BOXES, STAIRS—INT., NIGHT

Leaving their box, Dora and Rodolfo mix with the rest of the audience going toward the staircase and exit. Their friends are up ahead.

DORA

I'm so glad I came. It's put me in a good mood. Let's go for a chocolate ice cream.

RODOLFO

Okay, but we'll have to be quick.

DORA

Why?

RODOLFO

We have to be at the prefect's at eight. We were invited
to dinner.

DORA

Where?

Rodolfo is exaggeratedly patient, speaking in a low voice while he smiles left and right.

RODOLFO

At the prefect's!

DORA *(to herself, disappointed)*

Oh, Lord! Say it isn't so. Another dinner at the prefect's?

RODOLFO

Your mother's coming too.

DORA

Bingo. I am not going to the prefect's!

RODOLFO

Okay, dinner, just the two of us. We can stop at the
prefect's afterwards for coffee.

DORA

I am not coming.

RODOLFO

Fine, I get it. I'll tell him we're not going. It's just you and
me.

*They begin descending the stairs, and meet the PREFECT and his wife: He is all dolled
up, she is covered in jewels.*

PREFECT *(cordially)*

Good evening, Rodolfo.
　　　　　(to Dora)

Signorina.

All smile.

RODOLFO

Good evening, Prefect!

PREFECT

So I will expect you shortly. See you at eight.

RODOLFO (*intimidated*)

We'll be there at eight o'clock sharp.

The prefect and his wife go downstairs ahead of the couple. Dora doesn't move. Rodolfo turns to give her his hand, and she sneaks him a kick in the shin.

RODOLFO

Ow!

Scene 22

THE THEATER'S MAIN ENTRANCE—INT., NIGHT

It is thundering. The entrance is crowded with theatergoers seeking shelter from the rain and waiting until it lets up a little. Some dart out into the downpour. Guido is with Ferruccio, near the coatroom. He stands on tiptoe, looking for Dora.

GUIDO

Where is she? Have you seen her?

The upholsterer, all dressed up, approaches them. He is with his wife.

UPHOLSTERER (*to Ferruccio*)

You? Here?

GUIDO

How are you?

UPHOLSTERER
Right on time tomorrow, okay?

Ferruccio nods and smiles at the upholsterer's wife.

UPHOLSTERER
Did you unload that stuff from the car? That's silk, I don't
want it ruined.

The coatroom attendant puts the upholsterer's raincoat and hat on the counter.

UPHOLSTERER
Nice production, wasn't it?

Guido sees the upholsterer's hat and immediately decides to play his usual game: He reaches for the curtains on the wall.

GUIDO
A great production! Did you do these curtains?

The upholsterer turns to look, and Guido exchanges the hats: He puts on the upholsterer's and leaves his own on the raincoat.

UPHOLSTERER
Which? No, I didn't do these.

Guido pulls Ferruccio into the crowd. The upholsterer turns, but can't find them. He notices the hat switch.

UPHOLSTERER
He took my hat!

Scene 23

THE THEATER ENTRANCE—EXT., NIGHT

It is still pouring. Dora and Rodolfo are standing on the doorstep. She steps back.

RODOLFO

Come on, let's go.

DORA

It's raining too hard. You go get the car.

RODOLFO

Okay, okay. Wait here, I'll stop in front and honk the
horn.

*Guido has heard the conversation. He has a sly look in his eye. As Rodolfo runs out
into the rain, Guido turns to Ferruccio and says excitedly,*

GUIDO

Give me the keys! Give me the keys!

Ferruccio gives him the house key.

GUIDO

Not the house key, the car key! Hurry!

Ferruccio takes the car key out of his pocket, but he is worried.

FERRUCCIO

The car key? Are you nuts?

Guido grabs the key and starts to move. But he turns back suddenly.

GUIDO

Keep him busy—the jerk the eggs fell on! Keep him busy
as long as you can! See you tonight.

Guido hurries out into the street by another exit door.

FERRUCCIO

But the car—there's—go slow!

He runs into the street and gets soaking wet.

Dora is waiting at the theater exit, trying not to get wet. She sees a black car waiting at the sidewalk, tooting its horn. She hesitates a second, then rushes out toward the car. She gets in, and closes the door angrily. The car moves off.

Scene 24

THE CITY; THE CAR—INT–EXT., NIGHT

Dora, furious, refuses to look the driver in the face. She tries to brush the rain off her clothes as best she can.

> DORA
> You could at least have come and gotten me with an umbrella!
> You're just plain rude. Look what a mess I am!

She takes a hand mirror from her purse and tries to make repairs.

> DORA
> If there's anything that makes me really upset, it's dinner
> at the prefect's.

She begins to hiccough.

> I knew it. I have the hiccoughs. I always get hiccoughs
> when I have to do something I don't want to do.

Guido is completely focused on driving. Rain is falling like a waterfall on the wind-shield and the windshield wipers aren't working.

> DORA
> Don't you know that it takes very little to make me
> happy: a chocolate ice cream, maybe two; a nice walk
> together and then whatever happens, happens.

She turns toward the man she thinks is Rodolfo.

> DORA
> Instead you—

She screams.

Aaaah!

She puts her hand over her heart.

GUIDO

Good morning, Princess.

She looks around and realizes she is in the wrong car. Pillows, pillowcases, and rolls of fabric are piled on the backseat. She pulls her skirt down to cover her legs. She puts the hand mirror back in her purse.

DORA

This is too much. You'd better explain.

GUIDO

No, you explain! First, I stop under a hayloft and you fall into my arms from the sky. I fall off a bicycle—and find myself in your arms. I go to inspect a school—and there you are again. I stop my car in front of the theater—and all of a sudden you climb in. AND you show up in my dreams. Can't you leave me alone? This is some crush you have on me! I don't blame you, but… Okay, I give up. Fine, you win. Where to, Princess? To the beach? Do you like the beach?

Dora is amused, and even more amazed. Her hiccoughs have stopped.

DORA

Yes, yes, I like the beach. But people are waiting for me at the theater. Take me back.

She laughs. But now it is raining even harder and Guido almost has to rest his nose on the windshield to see. The windshield wipers aren't working.

GUIDO

Princess, do you know how to turn on the wipers?

She gets scared and grabs the dashboard, staring straight ahead at the water running down the windshield.

DORA

Step on the brakes.

GUIDO

Have no fear, hang on to me!

A second later both start bouncing up and down. The car stops with a loud noise and the engine goes dead. In the sudden silence they can hear the heavy rain and thunder. The steering wheel falls off in Guido's hand.

GUIDO *(embarrassed)*

Uh-oh. It's broken.

DORA *(a moment later)*

Forgive me for asking, but when did you learn to drive?

GUIDO

Me? Uh, about ten minutes ago.

DORA

Oh. I'd have said less.

*S*cene 25

THE CITY; STEPS; THE CAR–EXT.–INT., NIGHT

The car is stuck between two small stone pillars at the top of a long set of marble steps, in front of a church. At the foot of the steps is an empty square. Rain is beating down. The car doors can't be opened because they are stuck against the pillars. It is pouring on Guido and Dora's heads because the crash has unhinged the car's convertible top.

GUIDO

GUIDO

Don't worry, Princess, we'll get out of this. The
important thing is not to get wet.

*He grabs a large pillow from the backseat, takes off the pillowcase, which is embroi-
dered with heraldic symbols in gold thread, and puts it over the steering wheel and
shaft, creating a makeshift umbrella. The convertible top pops completely open; he
holds the pillow over Dora. It is pouring cats and dogs on Guido.*

GUIDO

Yikes, it's freezing!

*He gives her the makeshift umbrella, jumps out of the car, and runs around to Dora's
side. She climbs onto the backseat, holding the "umbrella"; he is going to help her get
out of the car, and she is about to set foot on the ground, but Guido stops her, because
the car is standing in a deep puddle.*

GUIDO

Stop, Princess! It's a lake here, you'll get your feet wet!

*In a flash he takes the heavy roll of colored silk from the back seat and starts unravel-
ing it on the ground. It unravels all the way down the marble steps, onto the square
below, and up to the portico, like a royal red carpet. Now a real princess can step out of
the car. Guido takes the "umbrella" and holds it over her head as Dora jumps down
onto the silk carpet. But her skirt gets caught in the convertible top's broken hinge and
rips to her waist, so her gorgeous legs and pantied behind are showing. But in the com-
motion and loud rain, neither Guido nor Dora realize what's happened.*

*Guido accompanies Dora along the red carpet, holding the "umbrella" by the steering
wheel shaft.*

*When they finally get to the portico, he is as soaked as a drowned rat, but her clothes
are hardly wet.*

DORA

Where are we? What piazza is this?

GUIDO

What? Don't you recognize it? We've been here together
before.

DORA

You and I? When?

GUIDO

What do you mean, when? When the car got stuck and it
was pouring and I made you an umbrella with the
pillowcase. Remember?

He puts the funny "umbrella" on his shoulder and dances a little waltz around her.

GUIDO

It was a beautiful night. I put the steering wheel on my
shoulder and danced a little waltz around you three
times, and when I stopped in front of you, you kissed me!

*He waltzes around three times, humming the Barcarole. And stops in front of her. They
stand stock-still a moment, but in his comical go-round Guido has noticed that Dora's
skirt is ripped to the waist in back. He takes another look behind her and goes dead serious.*

GUIDO

Princess, your behind is blowing in the wind!

She has no idea what he's talking about, then she puts her hands behind her and backs up until she is leaning back against the wall. She looks around, distressed.

Scene 26

THE CITY; UNDER THE PORTICOES—EXT., NIGHT

It has nearly stopped raining. Dora and Guido are strolling under the porticoes. He has the steering wheel resting on his shoulder and she is holding the pillow behind her, covering her behind.

DORA

It depends on the person. My father was like that. Oh, he could get me to do anything. He understood me, he knew how to handle me. And I was putty in his hands. I always said yes to him!

Guido stops and stands in front of her, right under the window where the workman always calls for Maria to throw him the key.

GUIDO

So all these treasures hidden inside you—is there a way to open the treasure chest and get you to say yes?

DORA *(smiling)*

It's easier than you think—all you need is the right key!

GUIDO

And where is this key?

DORA

Heaven knows!

She looks up at the sky, which is filled with drifting clouds.

DORA

It's clearing up.

Guido glances quickly at the main door in the building where the workman always stops.

GUIDO

So, this key that makes you say yes has to come from heaven.

DORA

I'm afraid so.

GUIDO

I'll give it a try. Maybe the Madonna will throw it down to me.

He joins his hands as if in prayer, and raises them over his head.

GUIDO (*shouting*)

Maria! The key!

A second later a key comes flying out the window and Guido catches it in midair.

GUIDO

Is this it?

Dora is amazed—breathless. She looks up, then looks at the key in Guido's hand.

Almost running to take advantage of the brief truce in the weather, they cut across the piazza and start down a boulevard.

Scene 27
___
THE CITY; THE PORTICOES—EXT., NIGHT

> GUIDO
> Do you really have to go home? What about the ice cream? The chocolate ice cream? We can get it right away.

> DORA
> No, not now.

> GUIDO
> Then when?

> DORA
> I don't know.

Guido looks up at the sky.

> GUIDO
> Should we let heaven decide?

> DORA (cautiously)
> No, leave the Madonna alone, I beg you! Don't bother her over a chocolate ice cream.

Guido sees Dr. Lessing, come out of a cafe across the street. He is with a friend, and seems happy. The doctor sees him and leaves his friend for a moment to stride over to Guido.

GUIDO (*to Dora*)
Since we can't decide on our own when to get this
chocolate ice cream, I'll have to ask.

He joins his hands and raises them over his head.

GUIDO
Maria! Send someone to tell us how long we need to wait
to get our ice cream!

Dr. Lessing stops in front of them.

DR. LESSING
Seven seconds!

He bows to Dora and moves off.

*Dora is about to faint. She smiles silently, the pillow slips from her hands and falls on
the ground. She does not move.*

Scene 28

THE CITY; DORA'S HOUSE—EXT., NIGHT

*Dora and Guido arrive at her door. The building is called the Liberty, and is sur-
rounded by neatly clipped box hedges and wet cobblestones. In one hand, Dora holds
the pillow against her behind. In the other, she holds a chocolate ice-cream cone which
she is devouring.*

DORA
This is my house.

GUIDO
I've passed it a thousand times and I always wonder who
lives here. I wanted to open my shop here.

DORA

The bookshop?

GUIDO

Yes. Then we could see each other every day.

Dora finishes the ice-cream cone and smiles at Guido complicitously.

DORA

Well, 'bye now.

She wipes her lips with her hand, like a child.

DORA

Forgive me, you've been so kind. But now I need a nice, hot bath.

GUIDO

Oh, uh, I forgot to tell you...

He hesitates.

DORA

What?

GUIDO

...that I want to make love to you so badly—you would not believe how badly. Not just once, but over and over. But I'd never admit it to anyone, most of all never to you. They would have to torture me to make me admit it.

Dora doesn't understand.

DORA

Admit what?

GUIDO

That I want to make love to you, over and over. But I'd never admit it, only if I were crazy would I admit that I'd

even make love to you here, now, in front of your own
house, for the rest of my life.

*He puts the steering wheel down, shaft first, like a cane, and leans on it. She stands still.
Thunder shakes the sky.*

DORA

Run, you'll get wet, it's going to rain again.

Guido takes off his hat to say good-bye, and water drains from it.

GUIDO *(saying good-bye)*

Princess...

Just then two bicycles come into view, and the upholsterer and his wife cycle by.

Dora realizes that Guido's clothes are soaked.

DORA

Your suit is completely drenched. Be careful not to catch
cold!

*Guido sees the upholsterer look over his shoulder and stop the bike with a triumphant
smile on his face.*

GUIDO

No, the suit's fine. It's the hat that's bothering me. I need
a dry hat. But where can I find...?

He looks heavenward.

DORA *(smiles)*

It's easy! How does it go?

She joins her hands and raises her eyes.

DORA (*loudly*)
Maria, send someone with a dry hat for my friend!

She has hardly finished her prayer when the upholsterer, without saying a word, stops alongside Guido, takes the hat off Guido's head and replaces it with Guido's old one. Then, very proud of himself, he goes back to his bicycle, which his wife is holding with one hand.

As husband and wife go along their way, the pillow falls from Dora's hands again. Guido picks it up and puts it back on the steering wheel to make an umbrella. It is raining again.

GUIDO
Good-bye, Princess.

Speechless, Dora retreats to hide the back of her naked legs. She is watching Guido as he walks away under the umbrella, dancing and humming the Barcarole.

Scene 29

THE GRAND HOTEL—INT., NIGHT

The party hasn't started yet. Guests are arriving in dribs and drabs in stunning evening dress. All the hotel's lights are ablaze, flowers and cocktail glasses shimmer along with the ladies' jewels. This is a modern hotel, built on a circular plan; the walls are frescoed with portraits of men and women of great class who seem to be conversing while they sip champagne, smiling serenely.

Guido, in his waiter's tux, is very happy as he crosses the room holding an enormous ostrich egg in his hands. But then he spots someone and becomes alarmed. He hides his face behind the egg and continues on his way. Rodolfo, who is with a friend, stops in front of him.

RODOLFO
Waiter, excuse me, where is the men's room?

GUIDO *(hidden)*

Straight ahead and left.

Rodolfo and friend walk on. Guido lowers the egg and continues on his way. He looks behind him: the danger is past.

Scene 30

DORA'S HOUSE—INT., NIGHT

The tidy bedroom glows calmly in the warm light of a night table lamp. Dora is in bed, the covers drawn up to her neck, but she is made up and her hair is done. Her mother, LAURA, a strict, if somewhat eccentric lady, is wearing a very elegant, midnight blue evening gown.

LAURA

If you don't get up immediately, I swear on your father's memory that I will never speak to you again for the rest of my life!

Dora's mother motions the maid to leave and goes to her daughter.

LAURA

I'm going to count to three now, and if you don't get up, I'll drag you up myself. One, two…and three!

She rips the covers off Dora, who is fully dressed down to her shoes and to the handbag on her arm. Dora hiccoughs.

DORA *(sadly)*

Let's go, then.

She gets up.

Scene 31

THE GRAND HOTEL—INT., NIGHT

Guido is thrilled by the beautiful people and especially the beautiful girls in evening dress. The orchestra plays lively music in the background. Guido is pushing a cart while turning to admire a young lady's decolletage. Then he does a swift about-face and instead of pushing the cart, pulls it. In fact, Rodolfo has appeared behind Guido, a glass in hand. A couple, friends of his, are with him. Farther ahead, as he nears the entrance, Guido hears Ferruccio call his name.

> GUIDO
>
> Do you know who's getting married? That jerk the eggs fell on!

> FERRUCCIO
>
> And the bride?

> GUIDO
>
> No idea. Everyone's waiting, but she's not here yet.

ERNESTO, the other waiter, joins them. He is out of breath.

> ERNESTO
>
> Guido...

Guido approaches him.

> ERNESTO
>
> Your uncle...something's happened. Come with me!

He goes toward the kitchen. Guido, worried, rushes after him.

> GUIDO
>
> Where is he?

> ERNESTO
>
> Outside, outside. The horse....

Scene 32

BEHIND THE HOTEL—EXT., NIGHT

Ernesto walks outside into the hotel backyard ahead of Guido. Robin Hood, Uncle's horse, is standing free of the buggy. Uncle holds him by the reins. The horse is painted green, with red paint on his lips, his eyes made up—and his mane is braided with colorful ribbons. On his flanks and thighs a thunderbolt and a skull are painted in black, along with the words ACHTUNG CAVALLO EBREO *("Attention, Jewish horse").*

> GUIDO
>
> Uncle!

He sees the horse and tries to minimize the incident as he helps his uncle tie the horse up.

> GUIDO
>
> Robin Hood, what did they do to you! Look at this—
> they made you up! Not bad—what did they write? (he
> reads) "Attention, Jewish horse."

> UNCLE
>
> Barbarians! Vandals! It's so sad. What nonsense. "Jewish
> horse." Did you ever?

Guido laughs to relieve the tension.

> GUIDO
>
> Forget it, Uncle. They did it to—

He means to say "play a joke," but his uncle interrupts him.

> UNCLE
>
> No, no, they didn't do it to...
> (he smiles)
> they did it to...
> (he turns serious)
> You'll have to get used to it, Guido. They'll start on you,
> too.

GUIDO

On me! What can they do to me? The worst they can do
is strip me, paint me yellow, and write, "Attention, Jewish
waiter!" Come, let's go, Uncle.

They go back into the hotel.

GUIDO

I didn't know this horse was Jewish. I'll clean him up for
you tomorrow morning, okay?

Scene 33

THE GRAND HOTEL—INT., NIGHT

*Dora and her mother appear at the entrance to the Hotel. Dora is intimidated. The old
porter, in uniform, accompanies her into the lobby.*

*Laura sees an elderly gentleman who seems to be waiting for her, and she rushes ahead
with a smile.*

*Guido comes down the staircase, very happy. At his feet, the party is in full swing. Voices
are lively, glasses clink, there is a crush of flashy clothes, jewelry, black ties and bare
shoulders. Ferruccio runs up the stairs to Guido, and stops in front of him, all excited.*

FERRUCCIO

Look! Look straight ahead!

GUIDO

Where?

FERRUCCIO

There!

*Dora, looking lovely, is standing with her friend Elena. In front of them is one of
Rodolfo's friends, dressed to the nines.*

GUIDO

Dora! Wait. I'll surprise her.

He runs down the stairs.

He is about to go to her, all smiles, but Rodolfo is also approaching her. At the last minute, Guido sees Rodolfo, grabs a vase of flowers from one of the tables, and hides his face behind it. He backs up like a whipped cur, hidden behind the flowers. Rodolfo takes Dora by the arm and walks away with her.

RODOLFO

Come, Dora, I'd like you to meet Fido Giovanardi.

Guido comes out from behind the flowers, lowers the vase, and sees Dora walk off and disappear into the crowd of guests. Someone calls him.

DR. LESSING

Guido!

Guido turns and sees the German Dr. Lessing, with an immense book under his arm. A porter is taking his suitcases out of the hotel. Still holding the flowers, Guido goes to meet him.

GUIDO

Doctor Lessing! Where are you going?

DR. LESSING

Urgent telegram, I have to leave for Berlin immediately. What are these flowers?

GUIDO

For you—for your departure!

He gives the Dr. Lessing the vase of flowers.

DR. LESSING *(laughs)*

I'll take one.

He takes a flower from the vase.

DR. LESSING

I'll bring it to my wife—a Guido flower. I really enjoyed myself with you, Guido. You're the cleverest waiter I've ever known. By the way: If you say my name, I disappear. Who am I?

GUIDO

Thank you, doctor. And you are the most cultured guest I have ever served.

DR. LESSING

Guido... if you say my name, I disappear.

He leaves the hotel. Guido stands still a moment, thinking, with the vase of flowers in his hand. The old, dignified porter, in livery, has overheard the conversation.

PORTER

What? What did he say?

Guido's eyes light up.

GUIDO

"Silence!" If you say it—if you say its name—it disappears! Silence!

PORTER

I was never any good at riddles.

GUIDO

"They bloom in springtime." What are they?

PORTER

Flowers!

GUIDO

Right! You win! Here!

He puts the vase of flowers in the porter's hands, and moves away.

GUIDO

I have to go to the kitchen. "Silence." Very nice.

The long table at which the engaged couple is seated is at the head of a series of medium-size tables. Sitting with Dora and Rodolfo are his parents and her mother, and the couple's closest colleagues and friends—including the principal of the elementary school and her husband and several teachers. Rodolfo is seated between Dora and Elena, Dora's friend, who could also be mistaken for Rodolfo's fiancée.

Dora is seated at the head table with her mother, Rodolfo, the principal, and a number of other guests.

PRINCIPAL

And not only in Berlin—even in the outskirts. In Grafeneck, in the third grade. Listen to this, I remember it because I was so struck by it. A lunatic costs the State four marks a day. A cripple four and a half, an epileptic three and a half. The average rate is four marks a day and there are three-hundred-thousand patients. So how much would the state save if these individuals were eliminated?

The listeners are startled by the problem. Dora is horrified.

DORA

I can't believe this.

PRINCIPAL

That was exactly my reaction, Dora! "Good Lord, it can't be!" That a child of seven can solve a problem like this? It's a difficult equation: the proportions, the percentages. Throw in a little algebra. For us it's high school material.

Rodolfo thinks a moment, then says,

RODOLFO

No, all you have to do is multiply! You said there are three hundred thousand cripples?

Yes.

RODOLFO

Three hundred thousand times four. Kill them all and
you save one million, two hundred thousand marks a day.
It's easy.

THE PRINCIPAL

Exactly. Very good. But you're an adult, Rodolfo. In
Germany children of seven solve the problem. It's truly
another race.

*Just then Ernesto, the waiter, puts a chocolate cake in front of Dora, but she is looking
in the other direction and doesn't notice. Rodolfo approaches and sees the cake.*

RODOLFO

Good morning, Princess!

Dora nearly jumps out of her chair. She stares at her fiancé, incredulous.

DORA

What did you say?

RODOLFO

Good morning, Princess. It's there on the cake. See?

*In fact, "Good morning, Princess" is written in icing on the cake. Dora looks around,
stands up, and a smile lights her eyes. She is about to leave the table when the orchestra
starts playing a peppy foxtrot. All the guests, without exception, get up to dance.
Only Dora doesn't move. Rodolfo puts an arm around her waist and guides her to the
dance floor.*

*Everyone's having the time of their lives. It's a great party. Red, white, and green con-
fetti float down in the air, covering everyone and everything. Seated at a nearby table
is Ferruccio. A little dog with ribbons tied in bows in its coat jumps up on his lap. A
very skinny young woman takes the dog back and asks Ferruccio to dance. Laura is
dancing with the prefect, and the two bump into another couple: the Fascist and the
principal. The soft, feather-light confetti falls everywhere.*

Uncle and the old porter in uniform are standing shoulder to shoulder next to each other. Uncle is looking at the frescoes on the walls, where elegant guests are captured forever in paintings; the porter, smiling, is watching the real flesh-and-blood guests at the live party.

Guido, a happy man, comes out of the kitchen with a tray in hand. He is looking for his beloved. The music stops and everyone applauds. Guido turns distractedly and sees, in the center of the deserted dance floor, Dora, standing next to Rodolfo, the egg jerk.

RODOLFO (*his voice raised*)
Thank you, thank you. Just a few words—although you
know it all by now, anyway; you've known it for some
years. Dora and I were born on the same street, we went
to the same school, and we had the same friends. We
have always been together. The only thing we didn't do
together was military service!

Everyone laughs. Above the guests' heads the tray that Guido is holding up in his hand floats like a periscope. Rodolfo speaks more quickly.

RODOLFO
In brief, Dora is the woman of my life, and I am the man of
her life. We're going to be married within the year, and you
are all officially invited: April nine, save the day. In the
Church of Saint Mary the Pilgrim. And then we'll party till
dawn, all together here again, as happy as we are now!
Applause.

BRUNO
Kiss her, kiss her!

Rodolfo's friends shout.

FRIENDS (*in unison*)
Kiss her, kiss her!

Tears shine in Laura's eyes. Ferruccio frowns. Guido moves off, holding the tray high over his head while in the center of the dance floor Rodolfo kisses Dora, who offers him her cheek. But the innocent kiss is followed by a huge crash. Everyone turns; it's only a clumsy waiter who has tripped and fallen. Guido is on the floor, spread out like a dead

frog amongst the pastries, cakes, and silverware that have toppled in the crash.
Ferruccio and Ernesto run to help him. They pick him up as the orchestra strikes up a
waltz.

ERNESTO

What's wrong with you?

GUIDO

Nothing.

ERNESTO

Are you all right?

GUIDO

Fine, fine

Uncle arrives, but Guido is already standing and cleaning up the mess on the floor.

GUIDO

Who put this armchair here?

FERRUCCIO

Are you all right?

GUIDO

I'm fine.

                    FERRUCCIO

I'm sorry.

                     GUIDO

I didn't get hurt.

                    FERRUCCIO

No, I was talking about…

                     GUIDO

Are you enjoying yourself?

                    FERRUCCIO

It's going fine.

                     GUIDO

Go back to your table. Go on, I can do this.

He stands up and starts picking up the mess as his uncle again approaches him.

Guido stands, with a poodle on his tray.

                     UNCLE

Are you all right?

                     GUIDO

Fine! Why are you all asking me that? Is there something
wrong?

                     UNCLE

No, nothing is wrong. But go to the kitchen.

                     GUIDO

Okay.

But he goes to the dance floor. As Ernesto finishes cleaning up, Uncle calls to Guido.

                     UNCLE

Guido, go to the kitchen.

GUIDO

They moved everything tonight. Look where they put
the kitchen!

Guido goes to the kitchen like a robot. Uncle's eyes follow him. Guido still doesn't real-
ize that the dog is on the tray.

The orchestra finishes a Charleston. The room is dotted with the bright colors of the
confetti. The dancers return to their tables and chairs. Dora, her mother, and Rodolfo
sit down at their places of honor at the long table.

A young man in a Fascist uniform, BRUNO, flushed and happily tipsy, moves
toward the couple. He stops behind Rodolfo, who is seated next to Dora, and covers his
friend's eyes with his hands, laughing.

BRUNO

Peekaboo, guess who? It's me! What, have you gone soft?

Rodolfo is surprised. He tries to take the hands off his eyes.

Bruno laughs, takes Dora's hand, and kisses it.

BRUNO

Young lady, we finally meet! Dora! We've never been
introduced—you were scared to, weren't you?

He whispers something in Rodolfo's ear.

BRUNO

I guess you won't be coming with us to the bordello
anymore.

He takes a step backward and raises his arms.

BRUNO *(loudly)*

Sorry to have bothered you—lots of luck and happiness!

He slaps Rodolfo on the shoulder.

BRUNO

You sly dog.

LAURA

What a happy fellow!

Guido comes out of the kitchen with a tray of confections. He passes Dora's table & drops the tray.

GUIDO

Don't worry about a thing, I'll pick them up. I apologize.

He looks around to be sure his uncle hasn't seen his latest catastrophe, then bends down to pick up the mess. This time Dora has seen everything, and sees him disappear under the table. Next to her is Rodolfo, who is talking with a friend. On her other side is her mother, who is talking to the principal.

LAURA *(to Dora)*

What was the name of the girl who married Remo, that rich guy with a limp? Marianna!

She turns to the principal.

LAURA

...She used to go out alone every night; smoked like a chimney. She took all his money.

PRINCIPAL

No!

LAURA

Yes, I tell you! I knew it the moment I set eyes on her....

Meanwhile, Dora is slipping slowly under the table. No one notices. Guido is on his knees gathering up the confections. He raises his eyes and sees an apparition: Dora, on her hands and knees, crawling toward him.

GUIDO

Princess, you're here too?

DORA (*with a half smile*)

Eh!

Without a moment's hesitation, she kisses him on the lips, a long, funny kiss. Their lips part and she turns serious.

DORA

Take me away!

She turns and crawls backward slowly. He watches her go, spellbound.

GUIDO (*to himself*)

Take me away....

Dora is crawling away, her behind facing Guido. She turns her head, smiles again.

There is a drum roll and a trumpet sounds; the musicians start improvising some vaguely African melody. Four Ethiopians, in colorful native costume, come down the stairs carrying a large tray on their shoulders. On the tray is the immense Ethiopian cake. The orchestra leader is speaking at the microphone.

ORCHESTRA LEADER

And now, a superb show, courtesy of the hotel management: Ethiopian cake!

Applause.

The Africans go toward the dais, but the orchestra, resuming play, catches sight of something taking place in the other direction and their music slowly dies away. A man who has been shaking a bottle of champagne stops.

Coming through the main entrance is a man wearing a tuxedo; he is seated on a green horse. It is an unreal image. On the mare the words, ATTENTION, JEWISH HORSE are painted. Guido is in the saddle, smiling broadly.

Everyone, caught unaware by the sight, is breathless. The horseman makes the rounds of the room. He passes in front of the musicians, takes the bottle of champagne from the hands of the gentleman who was uncorking it, and gestures to the orchestra.

GUIDO

Music, Maestro!

The orchestra leader, amused because he thinks this is part of the hotel's entertainment (as do most of the guests), waves his baton. The music starts, even louder than before.

Ferruccio jumps to his feet. He has the little dog in his hand; it is barking.

The dog runs away; Ferruccio grabs it again.

Uncle, who is pouring cognac into a glass, stops and drinks cognac from the bottle.

Guido and the horse finish their tour of the room and stop before the guests of honor. The music stops. Guido extends his hand to Dora.

GUIDO

Congratulations.

RODOLOFO

Thank you.

GUIDO

Come, Princess!

Dora is excited and frightened. She hesitates, but only for a moment. Rodolfo stares at the horseman, deeply suspicious.

RODOLFO

Aren't you...?

GUIDO (to Dora)

Quick, Princess!

She steps onto the chair and then onto the table, then settles herself on the horse in her knight's arms. Guido offers the bottle of champagne to Rodolfo.

Rodolfo takes the bottle and holds it distractedly, wondering where he has seen this man. Everyone around him is still convinced that this is part of the hotel's entertainment.

Uncle is standing in the background, next to the Africans who are holding the Ethiopian cake on their shoulders. He is just a step from Rodolfo. Noting Dora's mother's and fiancée's confusion, he suddenly starts applauding. The orchestra starts playing again, a wildly happy tune. And the horse goes toward the exit.

As Rodolfo grows ever more alarmed, the cork on the champagne bottle in his hand is slowly rising.

RODOLFO (realizing)

That's...

He starts to stand; the champagne cork pops violently, shoots like a bullet to the ceiling, and lands like a bomb on the fake ostrich's neck. The enormous egg falls down...

...and breaks on poor Rodolfo's head.

RODOLFO (pointing at Guido)
That's the jerk with the eggs!

His face and clothes have egg all over them. As he tries to clean himself up, Rodolfo jumps furiously from table to table, going after the two fugitives.

The guests move aside for him, but just as the horse is crossing the threshold on its way out, Ferruccio steps in front of Rodolfo and blocks his way.

Rodolfo shoves him out of the way and runs toward the door, shouting.

RODOLFO

Doraaaa…!

He runs out. Everyone follows. The orchestra keeps playing. The four Ethiopians in costume are still standing absolutely still, the tray with the cake balanced on their shoulders. The ostrich is on its side on the cake like a dead bird with its beak wide open.

Standing next to them, Uncle is smiling.

Scene 34

UNCLE'S HOUSE AND GREENHOUSE.EXT., DAWN—DAYLIGHT

Guido is off the horse and is helping Dora dismount. They too are covered in green, like Robin Hood. The first, sweet hues of daylight lend an unreal tone to the scene. Guido goes to the door of the house and looks in his pocket for the key. He becomes increasingly anxious.

GUIDO

No! Ferruccio! Ferruccio has the house key, damn it.

Instinctively he shakes the door in the vain hope that it will open. Dora watches, amused and curious about the premises. She goes toward the greenhouse.

GUIDO

Wait. I need a wire. My father taught me. I'm a wiz with
wire. I used to make toys out of wire when I was a kid.
Here we go!

*He bends down to pick up a bunch of wires while Dora, curious, stops on the threshold
of the greenhouse.*

*Guido sticks a wire into the lock and starts working it. Finally it opens. With a smile,
he turns toward Dora, and sees her entering the greenhouse.*

*Guido decides to follow her; his heart is beating a mile a minute. He too enters the green-
house. The door remains open; from beyond it there is only a mysterious, otherworldly
silence for some moments until finally Guido's voice, loud and very happy, is heard
from inside the house.*

A Few Years Later

GUIDO'S VOICE *(calling loudly)*
Joshua? Joshua, let's go, you're going to make Mommy late.

*Finally JOSHUA comes out of the greenhouse door, preceded by comical sounds of
things crashing to the ground. Joshua is about six years old: He is skinny and lively,
wearing short pants, a clean shirt, and suspenders. He is holding a piece of string from
which hangs a small, tin, armored tank. He comes out the door in a rush, trips, falls,
and picks himself right up again.*

JOSHUA

I couldn't find my tank!

GUIDO

Don't worry we'll find it. Where did you leave the tank?

DORA

It's on the stairs.

GUIDO

Hold the bicycle. I'll get it

Guido goes to the stairs and gets the toy.

> GUIDO
>
> There, let's go.

He joins his parents, who are waiting for him next to a bicycle in front of the door to the house. Dora settles the little boy on the bike's handlebars. She sits on the cross-bar.

Scene 35

THE CITY STREETS—EXT., DAY

It is a sunny, hot summer, but people aren't very happy. There are few passersby; a woman hurries along the sidewalk. Every once in a while, a German army truck goes by, or a soldier on a motorcycle. The Orefice family bicycle comes into view, speeding along over Dora's protests and Joshua's excitement.

First one street, then another. But everything is different from the way it was before. Tragic, desolate signs of war are everywhere.

Shop windows are taped over; apartment windows are covered with heavy carton paper or newspaper.

The city's public statues and monuments have been wrapped protectively in old mattresses bound with string. Sandbags are piled between the columns of the porticoes.

Strange, foreboding posters showing helmets, skulls, swastikas, and rifles and urging final victory have been tacked up on the walls by the regime.

> JOSHUA
>
> Come on, Pop!

> DORA
>
> Take it easy! Easy! You're both crazy.

> GUIDO
>
> We'll be late for school.

JOSHUA

Go, go, go…

GUIDO

There's a horse! Two horses!

He rings the bike's bell like mad.

Scene 36

THE CITY—EXT., DAY

The square and the Francesca Petrarca school.

The bicycle's bell is ringing madly as the three crazy cyclists break into the square and head for the school's entrance.

DORA

Guido, stop ringing that bell, it's driving me crazy!

GUIDO

It's not me, it's Joshua!

JOSHUA

No, it's not me, it's Pop!

DORA

That's enough, let me down.

GUIDO

Here we are. See you tonight.

The bike starts to brake and stops in front of the school entrance. Dora gets off, and Guido playfully reaches for her rear end. She moves away, fixing her skirt. She walks faster.

Guido leaves with Joshua, on the crossbar now, ringing the bell.

JOSHUA

Go fast, Pop!

Scene 37

THE CITY STREETS—EXT., DAY

Father and son proceed on foot. Guido pushes the bicycle by its handlebars. They pass a small group of German soldiers. The two stop in front of the pastry shop. There are only a few pastries in the window, but there is a sign that says NO JEWS OR DOGS ALLOWED.

Joshua stops and stares...

at a pathetic-looking chocolate cake.

JOSHUA

Should we buy this for Mommy?

GUIDO

How much is it?

JOSHUA

Fifteen lire.

GUIDO

No, forget it, forget it! It's a fake. It's probably a fake cake like your tank. Let's go, Joshua.

Guido walks ahead while the little boy reads the sign. He catches up to his father.

JOSHUA

Why aren't Jews or dogs allowed in the shop, Daddy?

GUIDO

Well, they don't want Jews or dogs. People do as they please! There's a hardware store over there, they won't let

Spaniards or horses in. And what's-his-name, who has the drugstore—just yesterday I was standing there with a Chinese friend and his pet kangaroo. "No, no Chinese or kangaroos allowed!" He doesn't like them.

Father and son move off, backs to the camera, along the sad city street.

JOSHUA

But we let everyone in!

GUIDO

Yeah, well, starting tomorrow, we're going to have a sign too. Who don't you like?

JOSHUA

Spiders! And you?

GUIDO

Visigoths! And tomorrow we're going to write a sign that says "No Spiders or Visigoths Allowed."

He walks faster.

GUIDO (*almost to himself*)
That's it, I've had it with those Visigoths!

They turn a corner.

Scene 38
—————————

THE BOOKSHOP—INT.–EXT., DAY

Joshua is on his knees on a chair in front of a counter, and is drawing with crayons on a sheet of paper. He is reciting a nursery rhyme to himself.

His father is arranging books on the shelf: He is holding a pile of books in his hands, his chin clamped on the top book to hold the pile steady. It is a modest bookshop, but a happy one, and quite tidy. There are books and also notebooks, rulers, compasses, colored pencils...

A man with an arrogant air comes in; another man waits outside with a cigarette in his mouth. Guido greets the customer with a smile: He can't believe his eyes.

CUSTOMER
Good morning.

The books slide out of Guido's hands to the ground; he steps over them.

GUIDO
At your service! Everything half price!

CUSTOMER
Are you Orefice, Guido?

GUIDO
I am. What can I do for you?

CUSTOMER
Come with me to Police Headquarters.

GUIDO

Again?

JOSHUA

He's already been there.

GUIDO *(to the customer)*

What do you need me for?

He sees the man outside put out his cigarette by squashing it up against the shop window.

GUIDO

Is that man with you?

CUSTOMER

Yes. Let's go!

Joshua starts getting off the stool.

JOSHUA

I'm coming too!

GUIDO

No, no. You stay here, I'll be right back.
                    (to the customer)
It won't take long, right?

CUSTOMER

No, not long at all.

Guido takes his jacket from the hook.

GUIDO

Okay, let's go!
                    (to Joshua)
And you, careful how you treat the customers!

He goes out the door first. Outside, he greets the other man.

GUIDO

Good morning!

The man doesn't speak. Then the three men, Guido in the middle, move on. Joshua is looking out the window. Guido realizes it and does a funny goose step to amuse his son, then turns and winks at him.

Scene 39

THE BOOKSHOP—INT., DAY

Joshua picks up the books that his father dropped on the floor and replaces them on the shelf. He is humming his tune again.

His grandmother, Laura, comes into the bookshop. She is pale, her eyes shining with emotion.

LAURA

Hello.

JOSHUA

Hello.

She pretends to look at the books, moving slowly. But she doesn't take her eyes off her grandson, who is erasing a line on his drawing. She stops in front of him and stares at him. Joshua raises his eyes.

She picks up a book.

LAURA

I'll take this one.

She gives Joshua the book. He looks at the price and gives it back to her.

JOSHUA

That'll be five lire.

LAURA

It says ten lire here.

JOSHUA

Everything is half price.

She pays, and removes a sealed envelope from her purse. She puts it down in front of the child.

LAURA

Give this to your mother. Tell her it's from your grandmother.

JOSHUA

I never saw my grandmother, I don't know her.

LAURA

Would you like to meet her?

JOSHUA

Yes.

LAURA

Tomorrow you will.

JOSHUA

Tomorrow?

LAURA

Yes, because it's your birthday. Grandma's coming and she's going to bring you a very nice gift.

JOSHUA

A new tank?

LAURA

No, it's a surprise. Give the letter to your mother. 'Bye, Joshua!

She turns, and is about to leave.

JOSHUA
Grandma, you forgot your change!

She takes the money, staring at him. And leaves, still emotional but smiling.

Scene 40
_____

THE BOOKSHOP—EXT., NIGHT

It is dark. A few streetlights are lit. Guido is closing the store. This time, Dora is sitting in the bike seat. Joshua is on the crossbar. Guido closes the door.

DORA *(to Guido)*
When will you be home?

GUIDO
Less than an hour. I'm going to Uncle's to see if he'll
bring leftovers.

DORA
'Bye.

Dora turns the bike. She is talking to Joshua.

DORA
Then what did Grandma say?

JOSHUA
She's coming tomorrow.

He starts ringing the bell.

GUIDO *(to himself)*
It's about time.

Guido pulls down the store's shutter, on which is painted, in big letters, JEWISH STORE.

Scene 41

UNCLE'S HOUSE. THE LARGE ENTRANCE AND DINING AREA—
INT., DAY

Uncle's house has changed: Now it's a real house, serious and bright. Against one wall is the dining-room table and chairs. There are pieces of old furniture, an armoire, a broken-down night table, a chest of drawers, and different odd pieces. Another part of the room is the living room.

Guido is moving the table. Dora enters in a hurry, followed by Joshua. She has a painting in her hands, which she puts in a corner, then turns to her son.

DORA

And now it's time for your bath.

JOSHUA

No, I don't want to take a bath!

DORA

Well, you have to. Go ahead.

JOSHUA

I took one Friday!

GUIDO

Right! He took one Friday.

DORA *(to Guido)*

And you, change your shirt.

GUIDO

I changed it Thursday.

Uncle appears in the kitchen doorway, wearing an apron. He has a ladle in his hand.

UNCLE

Don't forget the flowers.

He goes back into the kitchen.

DORA *(to Guido)*
Didn't you pick them yet? Go do it now.

Guido goes quickly to the door.

GUIDO
I did pick them, I put them out here.

JOSHUA
I'm coming too.

DORA
No, you go take your bath.

JOSHUA
I don't want to take one!

DORA
Hurry up, I have to go pick Grandma up.

The child doesn't move. Guido goes toward the door.

JOSHUA
I took a bath Friday.

He goes out. Dora opens the armoire and starts looking through the drawers.

She goes into the bedroom and closes the door. Joshua stays in the living room. He sees the night table, which is bottomless and whose one drawer is broken, and gets into the piece of furniture through its front cabinet door, which he closes as Guido comes into the room with the flowers in his hand.

GUIDO *(loudly)*
Where should I put the flowers?

DORA'S VOICE
Leave them there, I'll be right out.

The wildflowers are tied with string. Guido puts them down on the night table, where Joshua is hiding. He turns to go, but hears a faint little hiccough. He turns and sees Joshua's hands and eyes through the night table's broken drawer.

JOSHUA

Shhh…I took one Friday.

Dora, hairbrush in hand and her hair loose, comes into the room.

DORA

Isn't Joshua with you?

GUIDO

No!

DORA

Then where is he?

She sits down at the table, a few steps from the night table, and starts brushing her hair.

DORA

Listen—come here, I have to talk to you before I go to pick up my mother.

Guido sits down next to her.

DORA

Hang the painting there—see if it looks okay. And where did you put the flowers?

GUIDO

They're on the night table.

DORA

Bring them here so I can see them.

GUIDO

Coming up!

He stretches his hands out toward the night table and wiggles his fingers. He has a mysterious look on his face.

GUIDO
Come, flowers, come night table. Schopenhauer, the
will. I want the night table to come here....

Dora, puzzled, watches him, then turns her head immediately, because the night table is rising slightly from the ground. Beneath it Joshua's feet appear. Then the night table moves forward in tiny steps.

Dora, over her surprise, understands the trick and smiles. But she is in a hurry.

DORA
This is a very dirty night table.

The night table stops in front of Dora. The cabinet door opens and Joshua appears.

JOSHUA
Good morning, Princess.

DORA *(loudly and sternly)*
Go take your bath!

Dora leaves the room. From behind the bedroom door, Dora's warm, happy giggles can be heard.

Scene 42
_____

UNCLE'S HOUSE—EXT.–INT., DAY

The buggy, drawn by Robin Hood and carrying Dora and her mother, stops outside Uncle's house.

LAURA
He can already read and write?

DORA

It's more than a year now.

LAURA

You've done a good job.

DORA

I'll help you get down, Mother.

Laura doesn't want any help, she gets down from the buggy with Joshua's gift in hand.

But something has already upset Dora....

The house doors are wide open: Smashed on the ground is Joshua's Pinocchio doll.

LAURA *(alarmed)*

What is it, Dora?

Dora doesn't answer. Going more pale by the minute, she goes to the door and looks inside...

...The table is still set, but a chair is toppled over. There is a broken plate on the floor. She steps backward, terrified.

Scene 43

ARMY TRUCK—INT., DAY

The truck's waxed canvas cover is burning hot. In the truck, people are sweaty, tired, frightened, and exhausted. They have been traveling for some time. They have luggage in their hands and laps, and are seated on benches. The children sit on the floor of the truck.

On the far end of the bench, behind the driver's cabin, are Guido and Joshua. Uncle, silent, sits on the bench facing them. At the other end of the benches, near the hatchback, two German soldiers are half asleep, machine guns on their laps and helmets in hand.

The truck stops and the engine is quiet. In the silence the only sound is the long, monotonous drone of crickets. Joshua stands up.

JOSHUA

Are we there?

Through the window behind the driver's cabin, Guido sees two Italian soldiers.

GUIDO

No, it's a railroad crossing.

Joshua sits on his father's lap and looks at a little girl sitting on the bench in front of him. She is petting a kitten.

JOSHUA

Pop, come on, tell me where we're going.

GUIDO

He hesitates, then improvises.
We're...uh, we're going to...what's the name of that place?...You've asked me a thousand times, and I told you: I can't tell you!

JOSHUA

Uncle, where are we going? I'm so tired...

UNCLE *(embarrassed)*

We're going...
(*But he doesn't know what to say*)

GUIDO

Joshua, what do you mean, "Where are we going?" Come on, didn't you understand what I told you?

Joshua shakes his head no.

GUIDO

Okay, what's today?

He smiles.

> Your birthday, right? You said you wanted to take a trip,
> didn't you? I've spent months planning this—come on,
> Joshua!

JOSHUA

Where are we going?

GUIDO

We're going...we're going...

He looks for an answer, but can't think of one. The child insists.

JOSHUA

Where?

Guido, with a sly, conspiratorial look, lowers his voice.

GUIDO

No, I can't tell you. You know, I promised Mommy. If she
finds out I told you she'll be angry at me. You know how
she is. It's a surprise. It's—it makes me laugh. My daddy
organized the same thing for me when I was little boy,
will you laugh! Look, first we're going...when you get
there, you'll see something and you'll say, "Oh!" but we
won't be there long. Then a bell goes...

JOSHUA

But where are we going?

*Joshua smiles faintly, then yawns. A fast train goes by in front of the truck, and when
it has passed, the truck starts on its way again.*

JOSHUA

I'm tired.

GUIDO

Go on, sleep a little!

A second later, Guido stares into Uncle's eyes with a worried and disbelieving expression.

GUIDO (whispering)

Uncle, where are they taking us? Where are we going?

Scene 44

THE TRAIN STATION PLAZA. A CAR—INT.-EXT., DAWN

Dora, tense, desperate, and speechless, is sitting in the backseat of a taxi. Outside the rear window is the peaceful countryside, caressed by the dawn sunlight. The driver, in smock and beret, slows down and stops in the plaza in front of the station. German and Fascist soldiers are standing guard. An armored car, a truck, and a German army jeep are stopped outside the entrance, which is patrolled by two armed guards.

The taxi stops a short distance from the door. Dora gets out.

CABBIE

Should I wait for you?

DORA

No, you go ahead.

She walks with a confident gait toward the station entrance, her purse in hand, as the cab drives away.

Scene 45

THE STATION. THE STATION MASTER'S OFFICE/PLATFORM—
INT.-EXT., DAY

Dora is sitting in the stationmaster's office, surrounded by electrical equipment, controls, and telegraphic apparatus. She is looking straight ahead out the window at a freight train stopped on the first train track. The sides of the train's cars are slatted and *the slats are nailed shut. But through the openings, heads are visible, and frightened glances.*

Farther down the track are the open cars. The new prisoners are getting in one at a time. But it is too far from Dora, and she can't see Guido, her son, or Uncle.

The new prisoners move toward the freight cars, pushed by German soldiers. Guido, Joshua, and Uncle are the last in line. Guido holds the child by the hand.

GUIDO

What time is it? Looks like we're leaving right on time!
What organization! You've never been on a train, have
you, Joshua?

JOSHUA

No. What's it like? Is it nice?

GUIDO

Fantastic. Inside there's all wood, no seats. Everybody
stands.

JOSHUA

No seats?

GUIDO

Obviously you've never been. Are you kidding, seats on a train?
Everybody stands, very close to everybody else. It's real fun.

They are approaching the freight car.

GUIDO

Look at this line. I made it just in time to get the last
tickets—it was a miracle. Come on, Uncle, let's go, we
don't want them to tell us we're too late. "Car's full, go
home!"

They start to board, but someone up ahead stops, exhausted.

> GUIDO

Hold it, we have reservations, stop right there.
> *(loudly)*
We're here! Easy, easy—here we are, we've got
reservations. Whoa!

The German soldier pushes him into the car.

> GUIDO *(smiling)*

Thanks!

Once inside, he rubs his hands together happily. They are the last to board. The freight car doors close before their eyes.

> GUIDO *(happily)*

All aboard!

Scene 46

INT. STATION MASTER'S OFFICE.

A German OFFICER who speaks Italian enters the stationmaster's office. He is in a hurry.
Dora turns.

> OFFICER *(in a German accent)*
Can I help you, Signora?

> DORA
There's…there's been a mistake.

> OFFICER
Mistake? Who are you?

> DORA
My husband and my son are on that train.

OFFICER

What's your husband's name?

He starts looking through papers on the table.

DORA

Guido Orefice.

The officer looks quickly at a list and raises his eyes.

OFFICER

Joshua Orefice and Eliseo Orefice are also on the train.
Where is the mistake? There's no mistake.

DORA

I want to get on the train too.

An ITALIAN SOLDIER appears at the office door and stands at attention.

ITALIAN OFFICER

Ready!

GERMAN OFFICER

Then let's go!

To Dora.

Go home, Signora, go home.

Dora doesn't move; her expression is hard. Beyond the window, an Italian soldier blows a whistle and shouts an order.

ITALIAN SOLDIER

Go, go—you can leave!

The train's engine starts up.

DORA

I want to get on that train.

The German officer is about to leave the room. He stops on the threshold and takes a long look at Dora. The train has started moving.

DORA *(implacable)*
Let me on that train!

The German officer sticks his head out the door and orders, in German,

GERMAN OFFICER *(in German)*
Alt—Stop the train!

The Italian soldier jumps to obey. He blows his whistle and shouts,

ITALIAN OFFICER
Stop! Brake, brake!

The German officer steps back and lets Dora go through to the platform.

Through one of the slats on the train, someone sees...

Dora coming out of the station office, accompanied by a German soldier.

JOSHUA'S VOICE
It's Mommy!

In the space between the slats, Guido's face appears next to Joshua's. Both are looking out. Guido is holding the child in his arms. Uncle's face appears.

They see Dora in front of another of the train's freight cars, not far from theirs, waiting for the door to open.

GUIDO *(in a murmur to himself)*
Dora...

JOSHUA *(happily)*
They stopped the train so Mommy could get on.

The long "livestock" train is standing still, waiting for the last traveler to board. It is Dora, who nears the freight car and climbs up. Two German soldiers close the sliding doors and bar them shut. One of the two blows his whistle sharply, and the train starts to move.

Scene 47

THE CONCENTRATION CAMP YARD—EXT., NIGHT

This is where the train arrives. The tracks end at a heavy iron and wood fence in the foreground of a large dirt yard surrounded by dank, gray-brick barracks with small, iron-barred windows. Brutal, white spotlights scan the yard. There isn't a soul in sight. A few shadows move in the distance, near the main gate, a massive cement structure at the far end of the yard. Barbed wire on the fences gleams under the roving spotlights, as if moved by invisible hands.

Finally, a tiny light appears in the distance in the opening between the two main gates. As the light nears, growing brighter and brighter, the sound of a train slowly chugging to its long stop gets louder and louder. Puffs of steam blow from the flanks of the locomotive.

Two trainmen jump down and disappear into the dark. The train is immersed in the silent night.

Scene 48

THE CAMP YARD—EXT., DAY

A German officer leans out the window of the top floor of a German army barracks. He is wearing an undershirt; his suspenders droop from the waist of his pants. He is drinking coffee and looking down at the yard...

... where the train is still stopped. On both sides of it, armed German guards, four per freight car, are opening the doors and setting up exit ramps. The sun is peeping through a brick wall topped with barbed wire.

The women exit on one side of the train, the men on the other, prodded by sharp com-

mands, threats, and shoves. *Mysterious messages in German are broadcast from loud-speakers scattered throughout the yard.*

As soon as he is out of the train, Guido, ignoring the confusion, hands the half asleep Joshua to his uncle and goes looking for Dora. But the women are on the other side. He can only see her from afar, through the open doors of one of the cars.

Dora is also looking for him in the crowd of men, but can't find him. She is distraught with exhaustion and blinded by the light.

Guido jumps up on one of the links between two freight cars.

GUIDO (calling)

Dora...

Scene 49

THE CAMP; GUIDO'S BARRACKS—EXT.–INT., DAY

In a ragged line, the men walk slowly alongside a gray wall in front of the prisoners' dormitories. Nearly all carry a suitcase, a bundle, or a bag which they must leave at the door of their assigned dormitory before entering. German soldiers check that order is maintained. The dormitories are squalid buildings with small, barred windows from behind which disheveled, white faces with large, spooky eyes watch the proceedings.

Guido, almost at a run, catches up to Uncle and Joshua, who are walking unsteadily. He takes the child by the hand; on Guido's face is an expression of the utmost calm.

GUIDO

So, Joshua, how goes it? You're happy, right? Get a load of this place. How are you doing? A little tired?

JOSHUA

Yes. I didn't like the train.

GUIDO

No? Then we'll take the bus home....
(*yells loudly to the others on line*)
Listen, guys, we're taking the bus back! The bus with seats!
(*to Joshua*)
I told them!

JOSHUA (*to himself*)

Yes, it's better.

GUIDO

I think so too.

At the first door, the Germans choose some prisoners, take their baggage, and order them to enter. When those barracks are full, the line moves on.

GUIDO

Look at that organization! Did you see those soldiers? You have to stand in line to get in. People try to sneak in every which way, but they have to stand in line outside, and the guards check everyone. Look, they didn't let those two in!

In fact, two prisoners are taken away mysteriously.

GUIDO

Don't worry, though, they'll let us in, I reserved! See, Joshua? We're going to have a great time!

JOSHUA

Daddy, what's the name of this game?

GUIDO

Right! The name of the game? It's the thing game, the
one I told you about! We're all playing, got it? The men
here, the women over there. Then there are the soldiers.
Then they'll give us the schedule. Not so easy, is it? No,
not easy. If you make a mistake, they send you right
home. But if you win, you get first prize.

JOSHUA

What do you win, Daddy?

GUIDO *(hesitates)*

You win—first prize! I told you!

JOSHUA

Yes, but what's the prize?

Guido is having a hard time.

GUIDO

It's…it's…

Uncle comes to his rescue.

UNCLE

A tank!

JOSHUA

I already have a tank!

GUIDO

No, a real one. Brand new!

Joshua stops, open-mouthed.

JOSHUA

A real one?

He is ecstatic.

No!

GUIDO

Yes! I didn't want to tell you.

JOSHUA

How do you get to come in first?

GUIDO

I'll tell you later.

JOSHUA

A real tank!

GUIDO

A real one!

At the next door, the soldiers make some prisoners enter, Guido and Joshua among these. But Uncle is forced to continue walking with the other men.

JOSHUA

Where is Uncle going?

GUIDO

To another team, it's all been planned.

He waves.

'Bye, Uncle!

As they enter the barracks, they stop, frightened. It is a filthy, nauseating room with dank stone walls and dull light coming through the small windows. Bunk beds, piled three high, line the walls around a small space in the center of the room where the new arrivals are crowded together. About half the beds in the room are taken by emaciated, silent young men aged by fatigue. Here and there, faces peek out from the covers, smiling in friendship and solidarity.

Guido has to recharge, because Joshua is about to burst into tears. He rubs his hands together exaggeratedly.

GUIDO (*pleased*)
Ah, didn't I tell you? Is this amazing, or what?
(*loudly*)
We reserved two singles!

He and Joshua go to the first free bed they find on the bottom row.

GUIDO
Quickly, or they'll take our space.

Father and son will share a bed, the first available bunk they find in the bottom row. The two bunks above are already taken. The little boy is sad—he doesn't like this place. He sits down on the bed, with tears in his eyes. His father sees.

GUIDO
Okay, we sleep here, we'll snuggle up. Joshua!

JOSHUA
It's ugly here, it stinks. I want to go to Mommy!

GUIDO
We will.

JOSHUA
I'm hungry.

GUIDO
We're going to eat, Joshua.

JOSHUA
And they're really mean, they yell.

GUIDO
They have to, there's a big prize, so they have to be
really tough because everybody wants that tank, Joshua!

JOSHUA

So what do you have to do? Can I see Mommy?

GUIDO

When the game's over.

BARTHOLOMEW, *a longtime prisoner, thin as a rail inside his striped uniform, looks down from the highest bunk bed and listens sorrowfully.*

JOSHUA

And when is the game over?

GUIDO

You have to get a—a thousand points. Whoever gets them first wins the tank.

JOSHUA

The tank? I don't believe it.
                    (*He whimpers.*)
Do we get a snack?

GUIDO (*surprised*)

A snack? We'll see. Let me ask, we're all friends here.

He looks up and sees Bartholomew, who has been listening to the conversation.

GUIDO

Well, look who's here! See who's here! It's what's-his-name....

BARTHOLOMEW

Bartholomew.

GUIDO

Uh, Bartholomew, has the bread and jelly man come by yet?

Bartholomew, his expression unchanged, nods his head.

GUIDO
I knew it, we missed him! He'll come by again, won't he?

Bartholomew shrugs his shoulders.

Just then an SS CORPORAL comes in with two armed soldiers. The corporal is a pudgy man with a stern air about him. He looks over his shoulder as though waiting for someone. But he's in a hurry.

CORPORAL *(in German)*
Any of you Italians speak German?

No one says a word, they are too frightened. Guido says in a whisper to Bartholomew,

GUIDO *(whispering)*
What did he say?

BARTHOLOMEW *(very softly)*
He's looking for someone who speaks German. He's going to explain the camp rules.

Guido promptly raises his hand.

BARTHOLOMEW *(very softly)*
You speak German?

The corporal motions Guido to come stand next to him.

GUIDO *(very softly as he moves)*
No.

Guido takes his place next to the corporal, who immediately starts yelling loudly at the prisoners.

CORPORAL *(in German)*
Attention! I'm only going to say this once!

He looks at Guido, waiting for a translation.

GUIDO

Okay, the game begins! If you're here, you're here, if you're not, you're not!

CORPORAL (*in German*)

You are here for one reason, and one reason only!

GUIDO (*in Italian*)

The first one to get a thousand points wins a real tank!

CORPORAL (*in German*)

To work!

GUIDO

Lucky man!

The prisoners are trying to understand what the corporal and Guido are talking about, but only Joshua gets it. He is standing very still, eyes popping.

The corporal points to the yard outside.

CORPORAL (*in German*)

Any sabotage is punishable by death, sentence carried out right here in the yard, by machine gun in the back!

He points to his own back.

GUIDO

Scores will be announced every morning on the loudspeakers outside! Whoever is last has to wear a sign that says "jackass"—here on his back!

Imitating the Corporal's gesture, he points to his own back.

CORPORAL (*in German*)

You are privileged to work for our great Germany, building our great empire!

CORPORAL (*in German*)

We play the mean guys, the ones who yell! Whoever's
scared loses points!

The corporal gets tougher. He holds up three fingers.

CORPORAL (*in German*)

There are three very important rules. One: Never
attempt escape. Two: Obey all orders without asking
questions. Three: Any attempt at organized riot will be
punished by hanging.
> (*loudly*)

Is that clear?

GUIDO

You can lose all your points for any one of three things.
One: If you cry. Two: If you ask to see your mother.
Three: If you're hungry and ask for a snack!
> (*loudly*)

Forget it!

CORPORAL (*in German*)

You should be happy to work here. Follow the rules and
nothing bad will happen to you.

GUIDO

It's easy to be disqualified for hunger. Just yesterday, I lost
forty points because I absolutely had to have a jelly sandwich.

CORPORAL (*in German*)

Obey orders!

GUIDO

Apricot jelly!

A German soldier whispers something in the corporal's ear. He nods.

CORPORAL (*in German*)

One more thing:

GUIDO

He wanted strawberry!

CORPORAL *(in German)*

When you hear this whistle...

He sticks his fingers in his mouth to imitate the whistle.

CORPORAL *(in German)*

...everyone out of the dormitory immediately!

Guido sticks his fingers in his mouth.

GUIDO

Never ask for lollipops! You can't have any, they're for us
only!

CORPORAL *(in German)*

And form two lines!

GUIDO

I ate twenty yesterday!

CORPORAL *(in German)*

In absolute silence!

GUIDO

What a bellyache!

CORPORAL *(in German)*

Every morning...

GUIDO

But they were so good!

CORPORAL *(in German)*

...roll call!

CORPORAL *(in German)*

                    GUIDO
Just forget it!

                    CORPORAL *(in German)*
Every two weeks you get a day of rest, no work.

                    GUIDO
Okay, it's tough, but it's fun, too.

The prisoners look lost—they don't get it. But Joshua is paying close attention, not missing a single word.

                    CORPORAL *(in German)*
That's it. Anything else you want to know, ask the veteran prisoners.

                    GUIDO
Yesterday, for example, I played ring-around-a-rosy all day. Today, I'm playing hide-and-seek. A million laughs.

As he is about to leave, the corporal turns and adds,

                    CORPORAL *(in German)*
And that's all I have to say.

                    GUIDO
Sorry, gotta run.

The corporal points into the distance.

                    CORPORAL *(in German)*
The work areas are there. But you'll figure out the layout here soon enough.

The corporal goes toward the exit.

                    GUIDO
I'm playing hide-and-seek, gotta go before they find me.

The corporal leaves, followed by the soldiers, who close the door.

After a moment or two, the new prisoners rally around Guido.

A YOUNG MAN

I'm sorry, but…

Guido goes to Joshua.

GUIDO *(to the young man)*

Don't ask me, ask Bartholomew, he knows everything!
Don't forget to tell me what he said too.

Everyone goes toward Bartholomew, who climbs down from his bunk.

GUIDO *(to Bartholomew)*

Later, tell me what the guard said.

Joshua's face has a completely new expression on it. He is absolutely convinced that all this is one big game.

JOSHUA

A thousand points?

GUIDO

I told you! We're going to have fun.

Scene 50

THE CAMP; THE FOUNDRY—INT., DAY

It is an immense, hot, noisy foundry. The prisoners, in striped uniforms, work inces- santly under the lazy gaze of armed guards and in the midst of molten metal, sparks, heavy machinery, dust, soot.... The place is an inferno.

Guido, his tongue hanging out, is on his knees, carrying a gigantic anvil and moving along ever so slowly. He takes a step and seems about to fall over. Suddenly, he finds himself in front of a staircase. It takes him by surprise. He stops and blinks. He looks up, studying the staircase. He turns to VITTORIO, one of his roommates, who isn't far behind, also carrying an anvil in hand.

He starts walking, swaying.

> GUIDO
> They're half crazy!

They go toward the oven doors.

> GUIDO
> This has to weigh one hundred kilos! It must be three
> thousand degrees in here. I can't do it, Vittorio. I can't
> cope anymore!

His arms pull him down farther and farther to the ground.

After only the first one?

Why, are there more to move?

We're here until tonight!

Slowly, Guido picks up the anvil, then goes to get another anvil.

Bartholomew is also behind him.

They stop in front of a mountain of anvils. They are surrounded by gigantic piles of iron objects that have been unloaded from freight cars.

Guido looks at the anvils.

Another prisoner is taking a piece of iron out of one pile. A straight razor is stuck under the piece, and the prisoner, pulling the razor free, falls backward. The blade goes flying and wounds Bartholomew in the arm. He falls to the ground with a yell, as a spot of blood appears on the torn sleeve of his uniform.

GUIDO

Bartholomew, what happened? Where are they taking
you?

One of the German guards rushes over threateningly, shoves aside the prisoner who wounded Bartholomew, and orders the wounded man to get up.

BARTHOLOMEW *(in German)*

To the hospital. I hurt my arm.

The guard motions him to leave. And follows him.

GUIDO *(to Vittorio)*

We're going to die here! I can't take it anymore! I'm
putting this down. I'll tell them I can't do it. What can
they do to me?

VITTORIO

They'll kill you.

GUIDO

Good Lord, I'll never make it. It's got to be ten thousand
degrees in here.

The guard points to the anvils.

GUARD *(in German)*

Work!

Scene 51

THE CAMP; BARRACKS—INT., DAY

Little Joshua is seated on the bed, waiting for his father to come back.

*The prisoners enter the room, wobbling with fatigue. They fall onto their beds,
exhausted. They are all present except Bartholomew and Guido. Joshua stares at the
open door. Finally Guido appears. He comes in, swaying as if drunk, but wearing a
smile.*

JOSHUA

Pop!

Guido, panting, shows him his striped uniform.

GUIDO

See this? Nice, right?

He sits on the bed where Joshua was. The child is now standing.

GUIDO *(panting but smiling)*
I signed us up. When I got to the desk the clerk said,
"No, you and your son aren't on the list! You'll have to go
home....You didn't pay your dues!" I almost fell over. I

said, "Get outta here! Joshua and I are already signed up. Give me a number!" And he gave me one!

Guido shows Joshua the number on his uniform.

GUIDO

Just to be sure, I had them stamp the number here too.

He shows Joshua his wrist where his prisoner number is tattooed.

GUIDO

I said, "Can I have a look at the tank?" He said, "No!" Fine; never mind. Are you happy now? So, did you play with the other kids today?

JOSHUA

Yes, but they don't know any of the rules. They said it's not true that you win a tank. They don't know about the points and scores.

Guido takes a piece of bread from his pocket.

GUIDO

They know, they know. They're just being tricky, don't fall for it. Everyone wants that tank. What, no tank? Are we kidding here?

JOSHUA

How many points did we get today?

GUIDO

Fifty! Actually, forty-eight, they deducted two points because I tripped while I was playing hopscotch. But I had a great time, I nearly died laughing. I can't wait until tomorrow. Hopscotch, tug of war, and ring around the rosy. Every game, I don't even remember all of them. "You guys are obsessed. Stop, I'm tired!" I said. Listen, did you eat something?

JOSHUA

Yes, but I didn't ask for any snack.

GUIDO

Excellent! So you got twelve points. I got forty-eight,
you got twelve. Wow—sixty points today! Sixty points
got us this bread. No jelly, though.

Joshua bites into the bread eagerly.

JOSHUA *(chewing)*

Sixty points? Is that a lot?

GUIDO

You bet! It's a lot, no kidding.

Bartholomew enters, in pain, his arm bandaged under his shirt.

GUIDO

So, Bartholomew? How'd it go?

Bartholomew's answer is to go slowly toward his bed.

BARTHOLOMEW

Couldn't be worse! Twenty stitches! Er, points!

Guido shakes his head.

JOSHUA *(softly, to his father)*

We got more!

GUIDO *(softly)*

Shhh. Don't tell him. We're winning! Eat.

THE CAMP; DORA'S BARRACKS; STAIRS; THE GAS CHAMBER—
INT.–EXT., DAY

The women, in prison uniforms, are being led down a steep, narrow stairway. They are all young prisoners.

In front of one of the rooms on the top floor, a strict German WOMAN ATTEN-DANT, in army uniform, stops an elderly woman who is about to start downstairs with the others. The woman is still wearing civilian clothes, however tattered.

> WOMAN ATTENDANT *(with a German accent)*
> Old women and children inside! You don't work!

Dora goes down the stairs with GIGLIOLA, a prisoner a few years older than she, a veteran of the camp. Her uniform is messy and torn.

On the floor below, a Second Woman Attendant is waiting. Next to her is an armed soldier.

> SECOND WOMAN ATTENDANT *(with a German accent)*
> Move it, girls! Faster! Come on—over here!

Dora and Gigliola go down the second flight of stairs.

> GIGLIOLA *(to Dora)*
> She's new, but she learned fast. The one upstairs who was
> shooing us out... she was okay when she first got here,
> but now she's the worst of all!

> DORA *(in a tired voice)*
> At least the old women and children don't have to work.
> Maybe...

> GIGLIOLA *(interrupting her)*
> Listen, the old women and children don't work because
> the Germans are going to kill them all.

Dora's hand goes to her heart. She stops, but Gigliola doesn't notice.

GIGLIOLA
One of these days, they'll call them for a shower:
"Children, shower time!" But the shower room here...

Gigliola stops at a window and points to a small, sinister-looking building not far away.

GIGLIOLA
...is the gas chamber.

Dora, next to her, looks out. There is a big, iron gate which is closed. An armed guard is outside. In front of the door is a long walkway, lined left and right with barbed wire.

The first woman attendant comes down the stairs at the end of the line of women.

FIRST WOMAN ATTENDANT *(in German)*
Lotte, open the other door! Let's go, let's go!

The women ahead of her go faster down the stairs. Dora, however, isn't moving. She stands, profiled against a window, looking out, her eyes filled with tears. The other prisoners are pushing her toward the landing..

Scene 53

THE CAMP; THE FOUNDRY—INT., DAY

Staggering, his tongue hanging out of his mouth, Guido is again carrying an anvil.

GUIDO
How can I do this? Vittorio! Where did they find these anvils?

JOSHUA *(softly)*
Pop! Pop!

Joshua appears from out of the shadows, where he has been hiding behind some machinery, and goes calmly toward his father.

Guido is panicked. He stops, resting the anvil on his knee.

GUIDO

What are you doing? You can't come here! Get back into
hiding, what are you doing here? Why aren't you with
the other children?

Joshua, staying in the shadows, weaves his way alongside his father.

JOSHUA

Because they said that today all the kids have to take a
shower, and I don't want to take a shower!

GUIDO

Go right now and take that shower!

JOSHUA

No, I won't! What are you guys doing here, Pop?

GUIDO

We're making...a...a tank. But we're way behind, we're
still on the treads.

The child wipes his nose with his sleeve.

GUIDO

See how dirty you are?
                              (sternly)
Go take that shower!

JOSHUA

No!

GUIDO

You stubborn thing! I'm going to tell Mommy! You'll lose
ten points! You wait right here for me, don't let anyone
see you, and we'll go back together. This sure is fun.

He keeps walking, until he is back in line with the other prisoners carrying anvils.

Scene 54

THE CAMP; GAS CHAMBER; WAITING ROOM—INT., SUNSET

Uncle, silent and with a faraway look in his eyes, is slowly getting undressed. He takes off his jacket and hangs it on a nail. The gas chamber's large anteroom is lit by a few wall lamps. Attendants and SS men check that all the elderly and the children are getting undressed.

> ATTENDANT'S VOICE (*in German*)
> Everything, take everything off. Get undressed and hang
> your clothes there. You'll get everything back after the
> shower. Remember your number to get your clothes
> back.

The second attendant turns, trips on something, and falls down with a cry. Uncle, his shirt already unbuttoned, reaches down and gives her his hand, helping her to her feet.

> UNCLE
> Are you hurt, ma'am?

She notices him for the first time and backs away, staring into his face with a frightened, upset look. Then she walks away with long strides. Uncle takes off his shirt.

Scene 55

THE CAMP; GUIDO'S BUNK—INT., NIGHT

Under the artificial ceiling light, the prisoners, in their beds, look even more ghostly. Bartholomew has moved into the lower bunk that was Guido and Joshua's. He is tidying up.

He has traded his upper berth with father and son, who now sleep in the upper bunk.

Guido prefers the top berth because Joshua can hide more easily from anyone coming in or out of the room. Joshua is climbing up, pushed by Guido.

GUIDO

Thanks, Bartholomew! Joshua, from now on you have to hide all day! If they find you, it's all over. They'll disqualify us.

JOSHUA

And what am I supposed to do all day?

GUIDO

Don't let anyone see you, especially the bad guys who are always yelling.

Joshua lies down on the bed and disappears from his father's sight.

JOSHUA

I have to stay here all the time?

GUIDO

No, no! I'll take you with me, don't worry! I'll hide you! This is the hardest part, because if no one finds you, we win the tank! We'll make a hundred twenty points a day on this one! You're not even here. No one's ever set eyes on you! You disappeared! Got it?

Joshua doesn't answer.

GUIDO

Joshua?

The little boy's smiling face appears.

GUIDO

Uh-oh. I saw you!

Joshua disappears.

GUIDO *(satisfied)*

Excellent!

Scene 56

THE CAMP; ONE OF THE STRUCTURES—INT., DAY

Dora and the women from her bunk are working in the shadow of an immense, dirty hut. It is pitiful, heart-wrenching work. Dora is standing in front of a big heap of clothing.

Her job is to separate hats, shoes, glasses, clothing, gloves—and put them on long portable tables made of planks and sawhorses.

She works with deep respect, her throat tight with pain, because she is afraid that any minute she will come across something of Joshua's or Uncle's. Amongst the rags, a little kitten is moving around, sniffing as if looking for someone or something.

Scene 57.

THE CAMP; A NARROW LANE; AN OFFICE—EXT., DAY

On top of a very tall pole, four loudspeakers are hung at right angles. A voice is giving orders in German to the army personnel.

LOUDSPEAKER VOICE *(in German)*
Attention, attention! The west gate will be closed for
several days. Heavy materials must be moved through
the camp's north exit.

In a long, narrow lane, a group of prisoners are returning from work.

Guido is among them, pushing a rickety wheelbarrow filled with empty sacks and all sorts of debris.

To his alarm, a little hiccough is heard every once in a while from under the sacks.

Around the corner, the group of prisoners passes by a door that opens onto a lit room. A German soldier runs out of the room and disappears down the street. Guido slows down abruptly; he's got an idea.

On the table inside the empty office is a microphone.

Guido doesn't think twice. He looks around, and as the last of the line of prisoners passes him by, he parks the wheelbarrow and goes into the office.

GUIDO
Anyone home? Am I intruding? Bitte!

There is no one. He turns and calls.

GUIDO
Joshua?

The little boy's head pops up from under the sacks—with a hiccough.

GUIDO *(in a low voice)*
Come here, quick as lightning!

The boy goes into the office. Guido switches on the microphone and taps it with his finger. The loudspeakers transmit the taps. He starts speaking, smiling broadly.

GUIDO *(loudly)*
Good morning, Princess!

Joshua approaches, very excited. He can't stand still—as if he has to pee.

GUIDO
Last night...

The loudspeakers atop the pole are broadcasting Guido's voice at full volume to every corner of the camp.

GUIDO'S VOICE
I dreamt of you all night! We had been to the movies....

Scene 58

THE CAMP; DORA'S WORK HUT—INT.-EXT., DAY

Dora is thoroughly stunned. She has no idea what is happening. The voice out of nowhere leaves her frozen. She steps toward the door of the hut, looking around, searching the air.

> GUIDO'S VOICE
> You were wearing that pink suit I like so much! And now...

All of a sudden, after some brief static, the voice changes.

> JOSHUA *(happily)*
> Mommy! You should see! Pop takes me around in a wheelbarrow, and he can't drive! You'd die laughing! And we're winning. How many points did we get today, Pop?

> GUIDO'S VOICE *(interrupting)*
> Quick! Run! The bad guys, the ones who yell, they're behind us....

> JOSHUA'S VOICE
> Where?

> GUIDO
> Over there!

The microphone is still on; there is noise, static, the sound of running feet.

Dora has been listening apprehensively, her fists clenched tight. Her face lights up as the voices become incomprehensible, hard, and guttural.

> A SOLDIER'S VOICE *(yelling in German)*
> Who was that? Who was the idiot who...

With a click, the transmission is over. Dora, coming out into the sunlight, looks up. A light breeze blows her hair. Not far behind her, two other women look up into the sky.

Scene 59

THE CAMP; BARRACKS—INT.–EXT., DAY

It is raining out. The sky is gray. Guido is leaning against the window looking out. He is very thin, and tired. A grimy blanket covers his shoulders.

Joshua's voice startles Guido.

> JOSHUA
>
> Daddy, are they dry?

His father turns and looks up at the little boy, who is hidden in the top bed.

> GUIDO
>
> What? Oh—yes.

He quickly gathers up the clothes he has washed as best he can and dried in the open air and throws them onto the bed.

> GUIDO
>
> Get dressed.

The door behind Guido opens suddenly, and several prisoners, dripping wet and looking depressed, come in. One of them is Bartholomew, who sits down on his bed. Guido realizes that many have not returned.

> GUIDO
>
> Bartholomew, where's Vittorio? And Alfonso and the others?

Bartholomew frowns as a German attendant appears at the door, followed by armed guards.

Joshua disappears into his bed; his father is watching from the corner of his eye.

> ATTENDANT (*in German*)
>
> Everyone else out!

The other half of the prisoners file out. Guido is last in line.

Scene 60

THE CAMP; A LARGE, WHITEWASHED ROOM—INT., DAY

The prisoners, naked to the waist, are lined up against the wall for a medical exam. A camp doctor, in a white coat, is standing in front of them; on one side of him is a woman attendant in a white coat and on the other side a soldier aiming a revolver, ready to intervene at any moment. The doctor's back is to the camera, he is wearing white gloves.

The medical selection examination is taking place in a whitewashed room. In a distant corner, other army men are seated at a crude table littered with coffee cups and papers.

Guido watches the doctor approach with amazement. After a quick examination of the prisoners, the physician gives his verdict to the nurse, who writes it down in a notebook.

The doctor checks eyes, hands and feet, gives his verdict, and moves on.

Now he is in front of Guido: it is him, no doubt about it. It is Dr. Lessing, the man Guido knew years ago at the Grand Hotel.

But the doctor doesn't recognize him. He examines him quickly, murmurs something to the nurse, and goes on to the next prisoner. Guido screws up his nerve.

> GUIDO
> "If you say my name, I disappear."

The doctor stops; the nurse is yelling something at Guido.

> NURSE (*in German*)
> Silence!

Lessing has turned to look at Guido, then turns back, motioning to the nurse. He looks at the prisoner, the first prisoner he has looked in the eye.

"Silence!"

A slight smile lights up Lessing's face. He takes a closer look.

DR. LESSING

The Grand Hotel!

Guido nods. The doctor moves on, thoughtfully, to inspect the hands of the next prisoner.

DR. LESSING *(to himself)*

Guido!

He continues examining the prisoners, but calls to one of the men seated at the table.

DR. LESSING *(calling)*

Franz?

A subaltern leaves the table and goes toward the doctor, who speaks to him rapidly, pointing to Guido.

The subaltern approaches Guido and gestures for Guido to follow him. Guido leaves the line and goes with him.

Scene 61

THE CAMP; GUIDO'S BARRACKS—INT., DAY

Guido comes in, dripping wet. He closes the door behind him. Bartholomew breathes a sigh of relief.

BARTHOLOMEW

Guido, thank God! I was so worried. What happened to
you?

Bartholomew, who has been standing, sits down on his bed. Less than half the original number of prisoners is left in the barracks.

GUIDO

This is a loony bin! They're all crazy! The doctor, the captain there—I knew him when I was a waiter. He says they're giving a dinner here for the officers and their wives, and he told me I have to serve at the dinner. Maybe he wants to help me. He might get us out of here.
                    (He calls)
Joshua?

He gets down and looks around worriedly.

GUIDO *(to Bartholomew)*

Have you seen Joshua?

Bartholomew spreads his arms. A hiccough is heard from under one of the bottom beds.

GUIDO

Joshua!

He bends down and sees the little boy under the bed, eyes popping with fear.

GUIDO

Come out of there!

But the child won't move. His father pulls him out and helps him stand up. He dusts off his jacket.

GUIDO

Look at this, you're all dirty! Now, when…

JOSHUA *(unhappily)*

Where were you?

GUIDO

What? Oh—I was… I told you, I had to finish a card game.

JOSHUA

They make buttons and soap out of us.

GUIDO

Joshua, what are you talking about?

JOSHUA

They cook us in the ovens.

GUIDO

Who told you that?

JOSHUA

A man was crying and he said they make buttons and
soap out of us.

Guido bursts out laughing.

GUIDO

Joshua! You fell for it again! And here I thought you were
a sharp kid!

He smiles.

Buttons and soap. Right. And tomorrow morning I'm
washing my hands with Bartholomew and buttoning my
jacket with Francesco and my vest with Claudio...

He is laughing as he pulls a button off his jacket and lets it fall to the floor.

GUIDO

Uh-oh, Giorgio fell off!

He picks up the button and puts it in his pocket.

GUIDO

They make buttons out of people? What else?

JOSHUA

They cook us in ovens!

Guido stares at him and laughs.

GUIDO *(laughing)*

They cook us in ovens? I've heard of a wood-burning oven, but I never heard of a people-burning oven. Oh, I'm out of wood, pass me that lawyer over there! No, that lawyer's no good, he's not dry! Come on, Joshua, get with it! Let's get serious now. Tomorrow morning there's a sack race with the bad guys, and you...

JOSHUA *(interrupting)*

No, Pop, that's enough, I want to go home.

GUIDO

Now?

JOSHUA

Right now.

GUIDO

Its raining now. You'll come down with a terrible fever!

JOSHUA

I don't care. Let's go.

GUIDO

Okay, you want to go home, we'll go!

He gets onto the bed and folds the blanket.

JOSHUA *(amazed)*

Can we really go?

GUIDO

Sure! You don't think they force people to stay here, do you?
(*He thinks a minute.*)
We drop out, they cancel us. Too bad. We were winning, too.

He pretends to look for a suitcase.

> GUIDO

Some other kid's going to win the real tank.

> JOSHUA

Which kid? There aren't any more kids, I'm the only one left.

Guido jumps down from the bed.

> GUIDO

No more kids? It's full of kids, it's busting with kids.

> JOSHUA

Yeah? Where are they?

> GUIDO

Hiding. They're not allowed to come out. It's full of kids hiding. It's a serious game.

> JOSHUA

I don't get this game. How many points do we have?

Guido opens the barracks door. It is pouring outside.

> GUIDO

Six hundred eighty-seven. I've told you a thousand times, we're first. We're winning! But never mind, we'll drop out. Let's go! I saw the chart yesterday. We'll go anyway, though. 'Bye, Bartholomew. Joshua and I are leaving. We're fed up here.

> GUIDO *(to Bartholomew)*

The tank is done, it's ready. Clean the spark plugs off before you start it. Open the throttle. Otherwise the cannon will get stuck with the tracks. And the gun, did you see how nice it is? It came out beautiful! Lift the emergency brake before you move! Joshua and I are

going. Joshua wants to quit. We could have gone back
with the tank soon, but we'll take the bus today. Joshua
and I are leaving. So long, everybody. We're tired of this
place. Let's go, or we'll miss the bus.

JOSHUA
It's raining, I'll come down with a terrible fever!

*And he starts to move toward the door. He looks at the rain. Joshua is standing still,
confused.*

Scene 62
_____

THE CAMP; THE YARD AND THE OFFICERS' MESS—EXT.–INT., DAY

The four loudspeakers are transmitting one of Hitler's speeches.

*From several windows of the officers' mess swastika flags and banners wave. All
around the gloomy camp buildings are signs of the recent rain, and mud everywhere.*

A German car stops at the entrance to the mess. Two women and four beautifully dressed children get out. An officer and his wife greet them, smiling. With the officer is another man in civilian clothes. They greet one another and introductions are made. A second car is already standing in the yard and a child, slightly muddied but also beautifully dressed, is hiding behind it.

His friend, a smaller boy, runs to hide behind a pile of stones.

Several German children who arrived earlier are playing hide-and-seek. Behind the entrance door to the officers' mess, one little boy, eyes closed and hidden against his arm, is counting.

> LITTLE BOY (in German)
> Twelve, thirteen, fourteen.

Guido is wearing a waiter's uniform, several sizes too big for him. He is inside one of the drawing rooms on the top floor of the officers' mess, and is setting the table with two male German attendants, in uniform, and one female attendant. Hitler's voice can be heard through the open window. The others leave the room and Guido is alone. He goes to close the window and sees...

...The little boy counting. He then sees him run with another boy and hide in a doorway, while the other children, hidden here and there and ready to burst, peek out.

But it's Guido who bursts out with an idea. He runs from the room.

Scene 63

THE CAMP; GUIDO'S BARRACKS—INT., SUNSET

The room is empty. Joshua is on the bed, banging a spoon against the bucket on his head. When he hears the door open, he quickly hides under the blanket.

But it's Guido, out of breath.

GUIDO
Joshua? It's me, Pop! I have to tell you something
important. Come here!

Scene 64

THE CAMP; A CORNER AND THE YARD—EXT., SUNSET

Father and son are walking very quickly down a deserted path.

GUIDO
I've been trying to catch that little devil since this
morning.

JOSHUA
Is there really a little boy?

GUIDO
More than one—there must be two thousand, they're
like mice, they're everywhere. But they know how to
hide. They want that tank, darn them!

*They stop at a corner that opens onto the yard where the officers' mess is located.
Guido keeps Joshua hidden behind him, and looks into the yard.*

GUIDO
Stop! I think I saw him, he's right near here.

*A few steps away is a small hut with a metal door, about the size of a night table,
which may house the camp's water main.*

GUIDO
Look and see if he's inside there, I'll stand guard here.

Joshua opens the door and jumps back.

A BLOND BOY hiding inside also jumps back, and signals Joshua to close the door right away.

BLOND BOY *(in German)*
Shhh! Close the door, close it! I'm in here!

Joshua closes the door and turns to his father triumphantly.

JOSHUA
He's there, Pop! He's there!

GUIDO
Was he blond?

JOSHUA
Yes!

GUIDO
Yep, that's him, all right. His name is Swanz. He's been hiding there for three weeks. He was ranked second, and we've eliminated him! Sooner or later, I'll find the others, too.

JOSHUA *(softly)*
How many are there?

GUIDO
It's a wasps' nest, it's full of them, I told you! All hiding!

JOSHUA
But where are they hiding?

GUIDO
Everywhere, I said!

Just then the woman attendant who was setting the table comes out of the officers' mess. She is chunky and efficient. She claps her hands and calls the children who have been playing hide-and-seek.

WOMAN ATTENDANT *(loudly, in German)*
Children, that's enough. Come inside now. Children?

Children come popping out. One was hiding behind a wall, two come out of the trunk of the parked car, one comes out from behind the pile of stones, another jumps off a windowsill. Joshua's eyes are bugging out of his head.

JOSHUA
Pop!

GUIDO
I'll be darned, it's a real hideout.

He points to them one by one.

GUIDO
Gottcha! Gottcha! Gottcha!

He turns and takes Joshua away fast.

But the German attendant sees Joshua and thinks he is one of the German children. She points a finger and calls out.

WOMAN ATTENDANT *(in German)*
Little one! You, over there! Come here! I said everyone inside!

Guido stops dead.

GUIDO
Holy smokes! She saw us.

JOSHUA
Are we out?

The attendant is walking quickly toward them.

GUIDO

No. Listen, she's coming for you. This is where the silent game begins.

WOMAN ATTENDANT (*in German*)

Well? What are you waiting for? Come on!

GUIDO (*without moving his lips*)

You have to be absolutely quiet all evening! Swear it!

Quickly he dusts Joshua's clothes, straightens them, and buttons the boy's jacket.

GUIDO

Swear it!

JOSHUA (*happily*)

I swear!

He crosses his index fingers and kisses them.

GUIDO

They talk so weird, you can't understand a thing. But you stay quiet! If we get through this, we win! It's the last round, the silent game!

The woman attendant takes Joshua by one hand, brushing him off with the other.

WOMAN ATTENDANT (*in German*)

The dirtiest of all! Come on!

But first she turns to Guido.

WOMAN ATTENDANT (*In Italian*)

Why are you here with the children?

GUIDO

I'm here to...

WOMAN ATTENDANT (*in Italian*)
Quiet! Never speak, understood?

GUIDO
I swear it!

He kisses his fingers. They go toward the officers' mess. Before Guido runs off, he winks at his son. And Joshua winks back.

Scene 65
_____

THE CAMP; OFFICERS' MESS—INT., NIGHT

The German officers and their wives and children are having dinner. There are about a dozen couples and a dozen children between six and twelve years old.

There are two adjacent dining rooms; a wide, open door is between the rooms. In one room, the adults sit at a long table. In the other room, the children sit at a round table, some quiet, some shouting.

Guido is serving at the adult table. Dr. Lessing doesn't even look at him.

An office, temporarily serving as a dining room, has armchairs and sofas that don't exactly match.

Annoyed by the children's noise, a MAJOR, in uniform, rises and goes toward the other room.

MAJOR (*shouting, in German*)
That's enough! Peter, Gretel…Be quiet while you're
eating!

The children shut up immediately. Joshua, mute, sees that the others have also stopped making noise. He likes this game, it's easy. And there's food, lots and lots of food. Dr. Lessing finally looks sneakily at Guido. The Italian waiter goes to his table and puts some bottled sauces down.

The two exchange glances. The doctor purposely drops a piece of silverware. Guido rushes to pick it up. As he bends over, Lessing whispers to him.

>   DR. LESSING (in a whisper)
>   I must speak to you, it's very important.

Guido is bending over.

>   GUIDO
>   Where? When?

>   DR. LESSING
>   I'll signal you later!

Guido picks up the silverware from the floor and takes it away.

The children are eating in silence. Guido serves the portions on plates which the GERMAN WAITER puts in front of the children. When he serves Joshua, the little boy says,

>   JOSHUA (loudly)
>   Grazie!

The child realizes his mistake immediately. The realization is confirmed when he sees his father, frightened, staring at him. The German waiter and several of the children look at him oddly.

>   GERMAN WAITER (in German to Joshua)
>   What did you say?

The child purses his lips.

>   GERMAN WAITER (in German)
>   What's your name, little boy?

Joshua doesn't answer.

Guido doesn't know what to do. The German waiter leaves the room hurriedly, ignoring the plate that the Italian waiter is holding out to him.

Guido follows him and sees him go down the stairs. He goes back to the children.

A moment later, the German waiter comes back with a heavy-set woman soldier. They enter the room and stop at the door when they see what is going on in the children's dining room.

Guido, his finger in the air like a professor, is teaching the German children how to say "thank you" in Italian.

He puts a glass in front of one of the children, who says,

> FIRST CHILD
> "Grazie!"

> SECOND CHILD
> "Grazie!"

> GUIDO
> No, not "crazie," "grazie." Grrr…

In unison the children, correcting one another, practice.

> CHILDREN
> "Grazie." grrr…grazie!. Crazie…crrr…No, "grazi."
> Gh…gh…

With a look at the German waiter, the female soldier, dressed as a cook, spreads her arms wide. She is in a hurry, but she goes to Guido with a stern look.

> WOMAN SOLDIER (*in Italian*)
> I said you are not to speak to the children!

> (*to the children, in German*)
> You children eat. No talking!

She leaves.

From an old-fashioned Victrola's horn in the next room come the sweet notes of a delicate tango, background to the officers' and their wives' evening. Dinner is almost over; people are leaving the table and sipping drinks. Some are smoking, some laughing.

Guido looks for Dr. Lessing.

The doctor is talking with a lady, who walks away when another friend calls her.

Guido approaches. He fills his German friend's empty cognac glass.

> GUIDO (*very softly*)
> Doctor, my wife is here too.

> DR. LESSING
> Ah!

Just then the major, smiling, joins them.

> MAJOR (*in German*)
> Lessing, what's going on? You seem worried these last
> few days. Enjoy the evening.

Guido moves away, puts down the bottle of cognac, and goes to the children's dining room.

The children, quiet as mice, are having dessert. Joshua's mouth is so stuffed, he can't even swallow. His father bends over his shoulder and says,

> GUIDO (*in a murmur*)
> Easy, Joshua. Eat slowly or you'll be sick. We're in the
> lead and the game's almost over. We'll be going soon,
> Joshua! Don't make any mistakes now, okay?

He stands up straight and, moving away, winks at his son.

Joshua winks back, hiding a smile.

In the other room, several couples are dancing. The other guests are cordially conversing.

This time, it is Dr. Lessing who moves toward Guido. Guido sees him. The doctor purposely spills his full glass on a long table set up against the wall. He waves extravagantly at the Italian waiter.

DR. LESSING (*loudly*)

Here!

Guido runs up with a napkin and dries the table as the doctor turns toward him, his face impassive and thoughtful.

DR. LESSING (*softly*)

Okay, Guido, listen carefully.

The doctor looks around one last time.

DR. LESSING (*softly, but passionately*)

"Fat and ugly as can be, and all yellow—that's me. Ask me what I am, I answer cheep, cheep, cheep!"

Guido is paying attention. He stops cleaning the table, paralyzed.

DR. LESSING (*loudly*)

"When I walk, I make poppo', so who am I, do you know?"

Guido is astonished.

DR. LESSING (*loudly*)

The answer's the Ugly Duckling, right?

He looks at Guido, nodding his head, then interrupts himself, vexed.

DR. LESSING

It *is* the Ugly Duckling—but it's not! I haven't slept in four months. A veterinarian friend sent it to me from Vienna, and I can't send him mine until I solve this one! "Fat and ugly as can be"—it has to be the Ugly Duckling. But he said it isn't! So what is it? I thought maybe a platypus, but it doesn't say cheep cheep! The platypus goes *frrr... frrr...*

He takes a half step toward Guido.

DR. LESSING

I translated it into Italian for you last night. What do you
think? Everything points to the Ugly Duckling. Help,
Guido!

*Guido has stopped listening. Sadly, he feels his hopes crash. But the doctor, oblivious,
keeps mumbling.*

DR. LESSING (*to himself, in German*)
"Fat and ugly as can be, and all yellow—that's me. Ask
me what I am, Jack—the answer's cheep, cheep, cheep!"

*The record is finished; the phonograph needle is revolving around the empty space on
the record.*

Guido looks into the children's dining room.

*They have finished eating and all have left the table except Joshua, who is asleep at his
place, head on his arms.*

*Guido changes the record. He sees an interesting one, and puts it on. It is Offenbach's
Barcarole. On the opening notes, a couple begins to dance a slow waltz, holding one
another tight.*

*But when the song itself begins, Guido opens the window wider and turns the Victrola
horn toward the yard. Where it is night.*

Scene 66

THE CAMP; DORA'S BARRACKS—INT., NIGHT

*The poignant notes of the Barcarole travel on the dense, low fog that enfolds the camp
yard. This music is Guido and Dora's song. Now, the notes move through the moonlit
haze and through the dark streets of the immense camp, looking for Dora.*

*In the moonlight, the iron bars over the small windows shine brightly against the
stones.*

Dora has gotten out of bed, drawn by the far-off music. She approaches the window, opens it, and looks out. She sees the moon, outlined clearly against the night, brightening the fog just over the officers' mess, where the windows are lit up on the top floor. The music is coming from there. She understands that it is for her—a serenade for her.

Scene 67

THE CAMP—EXT., NIGHT

It is as if the music is muted by the fog. Guido is in the yard, at the officers' mess.

> GUIDO
>
> Okay, come on!

Joshua appears out of the fog. They rush off, but Guido, shrouded in the mist, is disoriented.

> GUIDO
>
> Here!

They disappear.

The fog lifts, they reappear. The camp's white searchlight roams over the walls.

They disappear into the fog.

> GUIDO'S VOICE
>
> Where are we?

> JOSHUA'S VOICE
>
> Pop, I'm tired!

They reappear near a sort of workshop. But the fog is blinding. Joshua is asleep in his father's arms.

GUIDO

Where are we? I took a wrong turn, Joshua. Oh, good—
you're asleep. Pleasant dreams. Maybe it's really all a
dream. Just a dream, Joshua…

He is roaming aimlessly, the sleeping Joshua's head resting on his shoulder.

GUIDO

Tomorrow morning Mommy's going to wake us up with a
nice cup of warm milk and some cookies. First we'll eat,
then I'll make love to her two or three times…

He comes out of the fog.

GUIDO'S VOICE

…If I can!

*He stops at a patch where the fog is thin—and the sight before his eyes turns him to
stone. Facing him is a mountain of corpses. Just behind the pile of bodies, the sinister
arm of a crane used to transport the dead bodies is sticking up into the air.*

Guido retreats and is swallowed up by the white fog.

Scene 68

THE CAMP; GUIDO'S BARRACKS—INT.-EXT., NIGHT

*Guido and Joshua are asleep in their miserable bed, arms around each other. But some-
thing is happening in the camp, something amazing. The noise of trucks approaching
and parking outside the window wakes Guido brusquely; he looks out to see what is
going on.*

Outside, the truck, turning, stops; it is filled with prisoners, all standing, all terrified.

*Guido covers the still sleeping Joshua with a blanket and climbs down from the bed. As
soon as the truck moves off, Bartholomew's and others' faces appear at the window with
Guido. A rough voice, speaking German, is heard over the loudspeakers.*

Bartholomew...

                    BARTHOLOMEW
Shhh....

They listen.

            VOICE OVER THE LOUDSPEAKER (*in German*)
Colonel Muller, report to Headquarters at once! Colonel
Muller to Headquarters! Lieutenant Grokemberger, to
Headquarters immediately!

Silence

                    BARTHOLOMEW
Sure. They're probably in Australia by now!

Bartholomew's eyes are bright with excitement and happiness. He turns to the others.

                    BARTHOLOMEW
They must have called those two officers to headquarters
at least twenty times. They're long gone.

                    GUIDO
What else did they say?

He looks out the window.

                    BARTHOLOMEW
You don't need to understand German, you can see for
yourself.

*Their faces are seen in the window from the outside. Against the glass, images of chaos
are reflected: men escaping, enlisted men on motorcycles, an officer giving abrupt orders
to a platoon that immediately disperses. Behind them, there is a small explosion.*

BARTHOLOMEW

The war's over. They're running away.

GUIDO

So what about us? What happens to us?

BARTHOLOMEW

Who knows? They've taken about fifty truckloads of prisoners away. Either they're going to kill us all, or... I don't know.

GUIDO

Where are the trucks going?

BARTHOLOMEW

Look, the important thing is not to get into one of the trucks. They leave full and come back empty. Where do you think they're going?

GUIDO

What about the women? What's going on? We should get out of here, split up, and take our chances. Don't even pack, just go!

There are sounds of distant machine-gun fire and dogs barking.

BARTHOLOMEW

I've been hearing machine-gun fire and dogs barking for the last six hours; they don't want to leave any traces.

GUIDO

Good-bye, Bartholomew—see you in Viareggio. We'll start our own business: an anvil company!

He climbs up the bunks to wake Joshua.

Scene 69

THE CAMP; A YARD NEAR THE OFFICERS' BARRACKS—EXT.–NIGHT

A strong wind is blowing through the camp. Father and son are snaking their way down a dark lane, trying to avoid the searchlight. Joshua's shoulders are covered with a blanket. They stop at a corner; the officers' mess is across the street, a bonfire burning in front of the building.

> GUIDO
>
> Joshua, they're really fighting mad this time!

> JOSHUA
>
> What? Who?

> GUIDO
>
> They're furious at you! Everyone's looking for you, don't you see? They're turning everything upside down to find you, they're even looking under rocks! You're the last one, the only one they haven't found! Boy, are they mad! Get down—stop!

He bends over abruptly.

> JOSHUA
>
> What is it?

> GUIDO
>
> Nothing. I thought…Okay, tomorrow the game's over and they're giving out the prizes. If you can just stay hidden tonight, we get sixty points!

> JOSHUA
>
> How many do we have now?

> GUIDO
>
> Nine hundred forty! Plus sixty makes…?

JOSHUA

A thousand!

GUIDO

First place! We win!

He looks around. In the wind, a soldier turns a corner.

GUIDO

Wow, they're really hunting you down. See where that
guard's looking? Boy, are they mad! No mistakes tonight,
this is it! Go hide in that box, quick.

JOSHUA

But that's where Swanz is hiding!

GUIDO

Who?

JOSHUA

Swanz, Pop! The blond kid!

GUIDO

Right! Swanz! They got him yesterday. It's the safest place
now, they won't look there again. Take the blanket in case
you get cold, I'll be right back, I'm going to put them on
the wrong track! Go—one, two, three—go, Joshua!

Joshua takes off like a speeding bullet and hides in the small hut, which is about the size of a night table.

GUIDO
I think I saw him over there!

He looks around and runs away.

Scene 70
_____

THE CAMP—EXT., NIGHT

Next to the barbed wire a mass of women is waiting to get onto the trucks. The wind is blinding.

Guido watches from afar; he moves in the shadows.

He can't get any closer: There are only women and soldiers there.

He turns back at a run.

Scene 71
_____

THE CAMP—EXT., NIGHT

Guido, pushed by the wind, disappears for a moment in the dark. He hides when the spotlight is about to catch him, then moves on.

He stops at a corner, where he sees the crane with its macabre steel hand hanging in the air.

Guido turns and runs...

...but trips on something, perhaps a body. He keeps running, turns a corner again. At his back is the constant sound of gunfire.

Scene 72

In a cloud of dust, Guido nears the box where Joshua is hiding. He opens it and sees the child.

JOSHUA

Pop, you scared me to death!

GUIDO

Give me the blanket. Are you cold?

JOSHUA

No.

GUIDO

Then let me have your jacket, too. I'll throw it up onto a tree, it'll throw them off track.

Joshua takes off his jacket.

GUIDO

You should see how angry they are, how they're looking for you!

He takes the jacket.

GUIDO

Okay, so long!

He turns back.

GUIDO

Joshua, if I should be a little late, don't you move, don't come out! You have to wait, don't come out until it is absolutely quiet and you can't see anyone for miles. Just to be sure! Okay? Now repeat what I just said.

JOSHUA
I can't come out until there's no one around.

GUIDO
Right! Stubborn boy!

He kisses Joshua on the forehead, closes the box, and runs off around a corner...

...where he stops, pulls his trousers up over his knees, and ties the blanket around his waist. But suddenly he hears a dog barking loudly nearby. He peers around the corner and sees...

...a German soldier walking a German shepherd on a leash. The dog is barking at the metal box where Joshua is hidden; its muzzle is practically inside the slot on the door. The soldier gives swift orders to the two soldiers with him.

Guido panics. He doesn't know what to do.

GUIDO (*mumbling mechanically to himself, invoking Schopenhauer*)
Go away, guys; go away, dog; go, go...

Little by little, the three soldiers move away, the dog's master pulling the animal behind him. Guido breathes a sigh of relief.

GUIDO (*smiling*)
Good for you, Ferruccio—it works!

He runs off into the darkness, wrapping Joshua's jacket around his head.

Scene 73
────────────

THE CAMP—EXT., NIGHT

The women are climbing up onto a truck. In the background white smoke and flames, rising from a tall smokestack, are blown through the camp by the high wind.

Guido's face appears from behind a corner. He is wearing Joshua's jacket on his head like a woman's kerchief. He retreats suddenly because the searchlight is approaching the street.

When it passes, Guido comes out, takes a few steps, and quickly climbs up onto a windowsill. He grabs an iron drainpipe against the wall.

The searchlight roves under his feet. He jumps down and sneaks up, in the dark, to the women standing in line.

He moves among the women, looking at their faces.

GUIDO

Dora? Anyone by the name of Dora here? Dora?

He moves among the women.

Scene 74

THE CAMP; THE WOMEN'S BARRACKS—INT., NIGHT

Guido appears in the open door. The women's barracks are empty, barely lit by the lights outside filtering through the windows.

GUIDO

Dora? Dora, are you here? It's me, it's Guido! I know someone's hiding here, is there anyone by the name of Dora?

A moment later.

A WOMAN'S VOICE

No!

Guido leaves.

Scene 75

THE CAMP—EXT., NIGHT

A truck filled with women is backing up into a street where the wind is blowing clouds of smoke.

The women in the truck see Guido's face appear among those of the women standing on the ground.

> GUIDO
>
> Anyone by the name of Dora here? She's Italian—it's my wife! Dora?

> A WOMAN
>
> Yes, there's a Dora. *(she calls)*
> Dora!

> GUIDO *(excitedly)*
>
> Dora, it's me!

He starts following the truck, which is picking up speed.

> SECOND WOMAN
>
> Who's there?

It is another Dora, a pale girl with short, light hair and blue eyes.

> GUIDO
>
> No, that's not her, is there another Dora?

The truck goes fast; Guido is running behind it.

> GUIDO
>
> As soon as you're out the gates, jump off the truck!

But they don't hear him, the truck is already far away. Guido is alone, heedless of how exposed he is. In fact, a WOMAN SOLDIER sees him and blows her whistle.

WOMAN SOLDIER (*in German*)
Over there! That woman!

Guido, realizing what has happened, runs off. The searchlight follows him.

The light stops at the wall Guido climbed before.

The searchlight passes the window; something is hanging from the window. The light moves back and focuses on a waving blanket hanging from the window.

The light widens and creeps up the wall. Guido is hanging from the drainpipe, blinded by the light. The blanket has slipped to his feet. Footsteps are heard approaching.

Guido lets go and falls to the ground, but he can't run because the blanket is around his ankles.

He picks it up and ties it around his waist as best he can under the murderous eyes of a German SOLDIER who is nearing him, machine gun in hand.

The soldier pokes under the blanket with the gun muzzle; the blanket moves, and he sees Guido's rolled up trousers and male legs.

He takes a step back, and aims the machine gun.

Guido closes his eyes and hunches over, but a voice stops the action.

A SERGEANT (*in German*)
Stop! What are you doing? Not here, take him to the usual place.

SOLDIER (*in German*)
Yes, sir!

The soldier points the gun barrel at Guido, motioning him to go first. The soldier follows.

They move off toward the women's area, near the yard.

$\mathcal{S}cene\ 76$

THE CAMP; NEAR THE OFFICERS' MESS—EXT., DAWN

Scattered gunfire is heard here and there in the camp. A few jeeps with officers aboard leave the camp at top speed through the main gate.

Guido, dressed like a woman, is walking ahead of the armed soldier. He knows there is no escape, and looks around him for a last-minute solution.

A motorcycle goes by. Guido starts. The soldier says,

> SOLDIER *(loudly, in German)*
> Straight ahead, move it!

They go a few more steps. Guido is still looking around, but he realizes that they are about a dozen meters from the box where Joshua is hiding. He can't risk it, he slows down and looks toward the child.

Joshua's eyes light up in the dark box, behind the slot. He sees...

...Guido, in comical woman's dress, who winks and smiles at him. Then Guido makes

a funny face and starts goose-stepping—the military high jinks Joshua knows so well.

Still hidden in the box, the little boy stifles a laugh.

The soldier gets nervous, he doesn't understand the kidding around.

SOLDIER (*in German*)
What the devil are you doing! Speed it up—turn right
here.

There is a building on the right. The two disappear around a corner. Two rapid bursts of gunfire are heard. A moment later the soldier appears, walking quickly as he shoulders his weapon.

In the meantime, the sun has appeared on the horizon. The wind is still blowing. A truck approaches, but this time it is filled with German soldiers. It slows down. Two of the soldiers jump onto the truck, throwing their machine guns behind them.

The truck leaves the yard, followed by two motorcycles and an army car.

The sun has risen even higher. The wind begins to die down. The last hundred or so prisoners straggle out of the camp's main gate. They are the weakest. They help one another. And when the last prisoner has left the camp, the camera moves to the box where Joshua is hidden.

A few moments of silence.

Ever so slowly, the door of the box opens. Joshua comes out and takes a step or two, looking around with a half-smile. There is not a soul in sight, not even a fly.

Suddenly, from not too far off, a noise breaks the silence, the deafening noise of an engine, a brand-new sound that gets nearer and nearer and louder and louder. Joshua stares straight ahead. The noise is deafening by now. Then, on a street between two buildings, an enormous green tank appears. It bears the white American star.

The creature moves forward, raising dust and heading straight for Joshua.

The treads stop a few steps from the little boy...

...who is standing still as a statue, his mouth wide open. He can't believe his eyes. He smiles.

All around, the air fills with the sounds of other American Army vehicles, jeeps, and motorcycles. A few words of English can be heard.

The tower of the tank opens and a young AMERICAN SOLDIER appears. He sees the little boy and smiles. He looks around the deserted camp, then focuses his eyes on Joshua again.

> AMERICAN SOLDIER *(in English)*
> Hi, boy!

Joshua stares at the gigantic tank, which is moving. He takes a step forward.

> JOSHUA
> It's true!

He's crazed with joy. Behind him, American soldiers are coming and going, weapons in hand.

> AMERICAN SOLDIER *(in English)*
> You alone, kid? What's your name? Can you understand
> me? We'll give you a ride, come on up!

He holds out his hand.

Without thinking twice, Joshua climbs up happily.

Scene 77

THE COUNTRYSIDE—EXT., DAY.

Broad fields, all in blossom, slope down sweetly toward the heavily trodden dirt road at the foot of the hills. The camp survivors are walking toward the road, following others who are walking in the distance. They are scattered, an odd group, walking unsteadily, too exhausted to celebrate. American Army officers and enlisted men in vehicles—motorcycles, jeeps—make their way through the prisoners crowding the road.

The view from the tower of the tank, moving along slowly, is panoramic.

Next to the tank's tower, alongside the American soldier, is Joshua, all excited, enthralled. He is putting a last piece of chocolate into his mouth.

The tank passes by the prisoners, many of whom stop now and then to sit in the grass by the roadside and catch their breath.

Suddenly, the little boy turns: The tank has just passed someone he knows.

> JOSHUA (*yelling*)
>
> Mommy!

The tank stops. The child jumps down and races back up the hill as fast as he can.

> JOSHUA (*yelling*)
>
> Mommy!

Running, he throws himself at his mother, who is sitting on the grass near a cherry tree. She falls backward, Joshua on top of her, kissing her.

> DORA
>
> Joshua!

VOICE OVER *(adult Joshua)*

This is my story. This is the sacrifice my father made. This was his gift to me.

She looks and looks at him, paralyzed by joy.

JOSHUA

We won!

DORA

Yes, we won!

JOSHUA

A thousand points! Couldn't you just die laughing? We came in first! We get to take the tank home! We won!

She is eating him up with her eyes; she lifts him up in her arms. And he laughs.

THE END